MW00414333

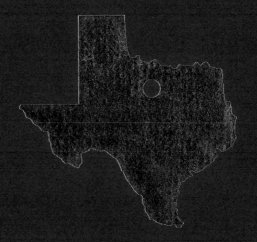

DELIVER ME FROM DALLAS

Also by Charles Willeford

Novels

High Priest of California (1953)
Pick-Up (1955)
Wild Wives (1956)
Honey Gal (1958) (as *The Black Mass of Brother Springer,* 1989)
Lust Is a Woman (1958)
The Woman Chaser (1960)
Understudy for Love (1961)
No Experience Necessary (1962)
Cockfighter (1962; rewritten and expanded version, 1972)
The Burnt Orange Heresy (1971)
The Hombre from Sonora (1971; reprinted as *The Difference,* 1999)
Off the Wall (1980)
Miami Blues (1984)
New Hope for the Dead (1985)
Sideswipe (1987)
Kiss Your Ass Good-Bye (1987)
The Way We Die Now (1988)
The Shark-Infested Custard (1993)

Short Stories, Essays, & Poetry

The Outcast Poets (1947)
Proletarian Laughter (1948)
The Machine in Ward Eleven (1963)
Poontang (1966)
Everybody's Metamorphosis (1988)
Writing & Other Blood Sports (2000)

Autobiography

A Guide for the Undehemorrhoided (1977)
Something About a Soldier (1986)
I Was Looking for a Street (1988)
Cockfighter Journal (1989)

Criticism

New Forms of Ugly (1987)

DELIVER ME FROM DALLAS

A NOVEL BY CHARLES WILLEFORD

20 01

FIRST EDITION
Published May 2001

Dustjacket and interior artwork
by Michael Kellner.

ISBN 0-939767-38-4

**Dennis McMillan Publications
11431 E. Gunsmith Drive
Tucson, Arizona 85749
http://www.dennismcmillan.com**

To Everybody

INTRODUCTION

ONE OF THE GREAT ONES
BY JESSE SUBLETT

"Man's unhappiness stems from his inability to sit quietly
in his room."   —Pascal

The above epigraph, which Charles Willeford used at the
beginning of *New Hope for the Dead,* came to mind as I mulled
over the odd events that led to my discovery that *Deliver Me
From Dallas!* was originally published in 1961 as a Fawcett Gold
Medal Original paperback entitled *The Whip Hand,* by W.
Franklin Sanders–mysteriously omitting Willeford's name.

The sequence of events began in January 1991, when my
wife and I and our two bad cats were living in Los Angeles.
My second novel had come out, and I was working on my
third while also playing in a rock 'n roll band with Mick Taylor,
the only guitarist who ever quit the Rolling Stones and lived
to tell about it. My usual habit was to write from about nine or
ten in the morning till early afternoon. I'd take a break and
then write until late in the night. Smoking cigars had always
helped keep me at my desk writing instead of wandering off
on strange errands and whims, but I had recently decided I
should quit smoking cigars. To bribe myself into quitting, I'd
taken up collecting vintage paperbacks. I figured that with the
money I saved on cigars I could buy one or two paperbacks a
day. This logic turned out to be deeply flawed, as I quickly
started smoking again and also found myself unable to quit
collecting books.

I soon had a huge collection of vintage paperbacks and
hardcovers, including multiple copies of all the editions of

Donald Westlake's "Richard Stark" books, all the Dell mapback editions of Dashiell Hammett, many Carroll John Daly first editions, and scores of books by hip hardboiled/*noir* writers like Jim Thompson, Gil Brewer, Dan J. Marlowe, Wade Miller, John D. MacDonald . . . and Charles Willeford. I became a fanatic. I had every Black Lizard paperback they published. And I especially loved Gold Medal paperbacks. That's how *The Whip Hand* came to my attention. But I passed on buying many copies I came across before I knew it had been written by Willeford.

Naturally, I was attracted to the cover, which has what we collectors call GGA–good girl art. There's a shapely blonde standing haughtily in profile to show off her missile-cone breasts, wearing high heels and gripping a bullwhip. The cover copy reads: "Lash by bloody lash, the she-devil from Dallas would get her revenge." At first glance, you might assume *The Whip Hand* to be another average to above-average sleazy sex and adventure romp, the kind that typified male fiction in the Fifties and Sixties. Well, *The Whip Hand* does fit rather cozily into that generalization; however, like many of the best works of previously mentioned authors, *The Whip Hand* offers more than a quick fix of off-kilter angles, gritty violence and poisonous babes. There's something beguiling beneath its apparent sleazy simplicity. When the events turn disturbing and funny at the same time, and when the plot spins on a point of absurdity and weirdness, it has the smell and feel not of a pulp writer's booze- and coffee-fueled desperation, but real life; as disturbing and funny and absurd as real life ever gets. This is the quality that Maura McMillan has so eloquently labeled "optimistic nihilism"–a quality that was one of the hallmarks of a writer who had a uniquely skewed world view, literary aspirations, and the chops to pull it off no matter what genre mask he appeared to wear at the time. A writer who, unlike many more conventionally accepted "literary" authors, never wrote a throwaway book. And I'm not talking about W. Franklin Sanders.

Charles Willeford wrote this book.

That's my opinion. Obviously, from the scant evidence available to us, W. Franklin Sanders was involved. Somehow. Maybe as a genuine co-writer. Most likely, judged by comparing their style and content, as is often the case in a collaboration, the two service buddies wrote alternating chapters, perhaps with Willeford doing a final "polish" to give it a more uniform feel. We'll probably never know for sure. What should be obvious to anyone familiar with Willeford's work is that this story bears the unique, unmistakable themes and gimmicks and quirks found in all his other writing. It's got his absurdist take on reality. The poker-faced, deadpan violence and sly, deadpan humor. The gabardine suit. It's Willeford, no doubt about it.

Like many Willeford fans, I came to his work late in his career. I first became aware of Willeford in 1987, when he was enjoying a belated taste of bestseller success through his Hoke Moseley novels–*Miami Blues, New Hope for the Dead, Sideswipe, The Way We Die Now.* Among fans of hardboiled/*noir* lit, Willeford is especially beloved for his lesser-known, harder-to-find works like *Cockfighter,* made into a great Monte Hellman/Warren Oates film in 1974, which sank into the same pit of near-oblivion as many of Willeford's early novels (2001 finally saw the movies' reissue on DVD). Later, after Willeford's death, came the film version of *Miami Blues,* which has its own strokes of keen brilliance, and the incredibly faithful and fabulous Rob Devor-directed version of *The Woman Chaser,* released in 2000.

It didn't take me long to become a bonafide Willeford aficionado, with my own quirky personal favorites, like *Off the Wall,* his novelized account of the story of David Berkowitz, the Son of Sam killer. Another prize is *A Guide for the Undehemorrhoided,* a self-published account of Willeford's hemorrhoid operation, with some other autobiographical segments woven in. I scarfed up all the hip reprints and special editions by Black Lizard, Dennis McMillan and REsearch Publications, and even set a few aside, so that I wouldn't feel like I'd run into a brick wall after having read every book of his I could lay my hands on.

That's why I felt so incredibly lucky for being a guy who loved to go exploring L.A. in his convertible Karmann Ghia, going jogging in the hills above the Hollywood reservoir so I could take a piss under the Hollywood sign, prowling used book joints, smoking cigars anyway, looking for the perfect *noir.* My daily journal entry for Tuesday, January 8, 1991 reads:

> *Drove through Lake View Terrace up into Little Tujunga Canyon, looking for Gary M's house which burned down after the SWAT team shot the wrong guy and then Gary shot the right one. Actually didn't find the house, but it was a sort of magnificent drive. Very strange area. A lot of people have horses up there. Next went to Vagabond Books in Westwood & visited with Craig & Dennis McMillan. Very cool guy, had a great time talking to him.*

I hate to sound cryptic but I really can't remember any more specific details about the SWAT team incident except that there was, I believe, a hit man and an ex-con involved. Naturally, as a crime writer I was curious to see the place where it happened. In any event, Vagabond, then located in Westwood, was one of my favorite places to look for books. I also enjoyed hanging out and talking with the inimitable Craig and Patti Graham, co-proprietors, whenever they'd let me get a word in edgewise. On this particular day Craig was behind the counter when I walked in. He greeted me with one of the cheerful ten-minute diatribe sentences for which he's famous, and then without pausing cocked his thumb toward another fellow in the store and said, "Jesse, meet Dennis. Dennis is sleeping on our couch for a few days."

The way I remember it, Dennis was wearing the coolest looking Hawaiian shirt I'd ever seen with a pair of fine fleck trousers and swanky two-tone Stacey Adams shoes. As I would later discover, this expression of sartorial splendor was the kind of casual outfit Dennis, the best-dressed man I've ever met, slips into when he carries out the garbage.

Craig hadn't mentioned Dennis' last name, so he and I conversed for several minutes before I found out he was Dennis *McMillan*, publisher of fine—make that extra-fine—books, like the series collecting dozens of out of print Fredric Brown pulp stories (*The Case of the Dancing Sandwiches* and *The Pickled Punks* among the twenty volumes in the set); reprints of a couple of Howard Browne's Paul Pine books; and most notably, Charles Willeford's *Kiss Your Ass Good-bye*, *Everybody's Metamorphosis*, and *New Forms of Ugly: The Immobilized Hero in Modern Fiction*.

That Dennis McMillan.

Naturally our conversation turned to Charles Willeford. Dennis knows how to talk—plus, since he'd known Willeford for several years, he knew tons of things about Willeford I didn't. We talked about other things, too, like flamenco guitar, which Dennis plays extremely well, by the way, and my own career as a rock musician, but we kept drifting back to Willeford. Two hours later we were still talking. Before I left, Dennis asked for my address. He said he was going to send me something.

A month later, a large box arrived in the mail. Inside were photocopies of half a dozen Willeford manuscripts. What a gold mine! One manuscript was a photocopy of Willeford's hardest to find novel, a Western called *The Hombre from Sonora* written under the pseudonym Will Charles (later published by McMillan under Willeford's name and original title, *The Difference*). The collection also contained a manuscript called

Grimhaven, Willeford's now legendary first draft follow-up to *Miami Blues.* Under that was a copy of Willeford's unfinished post-war Army/Air Force novel, *The Battle of Maldon* (it was to have covered a 24-hr. period in the "life" of an Air Force base in Newfoundland, but when Willeford realized it would take an 850-page plus book to do it right, he gave the project up).

The last one in the box was, in several ways, the most interesting of the bunch. The title page read: *Deliver Me From Dallas!* by W. Franklin Sanders and Charles Willeford

There was even a letter addressed to "Chas" from this Sanders guy. This probably sounds weird, but after reading the letter a couple of times, I decided the thing was a farce: that the double-author thing was a hoax, and that the letter was supposed to be part of the book, like the table of contents which followed, another unusual feature of a crime novel.

I read parts of the manuscripts, but mostly I just set them aside in a special corner of my collection, a secret treasure that I would savor on some rainy day. And I went on collecting vintage crime paperbacks. I specialized in early Fawcett Gold Medal editions. Gold Medal had published a lot of great tough guy writers in the Fifties and Sixties—Charles Williams, John D. MacDonald, Gil Brewer, and Wade Miller. And they had great cover art. One Gold Medal I became aware of during this period was a paperback original entitled *The Whip Hand.* Although I loved the cover, I passed on buying the few copies I ran across because they weren't in great condition.

I didn't see Dennis for several months. Something about going off to Hawaii to become the Howard Hughes of the Hawaiian shirt world—a story so ridiculous that, when it's a guy like Dennis, it must be true. Several months and hundreds of vintage paperbacks later, I saw him again, just briefly, at a book signing in Vagabond. One of the first things he said to me was, "Hey, did you read the manuscript about the woman from Dallas with the bullwhip?" I reluctantly admitted that I hadn't, and at the same time the ice machine at the top of my spine started working overtime. Something told me I had to get my hands on a copy of *The Whip Hand,* pronto!

I scavenged my local book haunts, and peered through the used book catalogues that came almost every day in the mail. No dice. But I did know a place that probably still had a copy, a small used bookstore up at Big Bear Lake, where my wife and I loved to go for weekend getaways (also, not coincidentally, where Chandler spent a lot of time, and used as the setting for *The Lady in the Lake*). On our next trip to Big Bear, we went straight to that store and I shelled out four bucks for a dog-eared, slightly foxed copy of *The Whip Hand.* I took it back to our cabin and compared it to the *Deliver Me From Dallas!* manuscript. It didn't take long to decide. No doubt about it: *Deliver Me From Dallas!* and *The Whip Hand* are the same book. Sure, there are differences–mostly line edits, a few different passages, different names, and a longer intro, but it's the same book. And what's more, it's pure Willeford.

Or, to be more precise, I concur with Betsy Willeford that there are portions of the book where I *know* it's Charles Willeford writing, and others where it seems it just *can't* be. The protagonist of the story, L.A. police detective Bill Brown, recently busted for taking bribes and demoted to traffic cop, exemplifies Willeford's unique style of black humor completely. The novel is written in first-person, but alternates between the voices of the various main characters chapter by chapter. The Bill Brown chapters, for the most part, sound like pure Willeford; especially the intro, which could hardly have been written by any other person. But Chapter Seven, written in the voice of Madge Baeder, a hooker, has the tone of a score or two average-to-above-average hard-boiled novels I've read; and that's a tone I've *never* felt reading Charles Willeford. Chapter Twelve, in the voice of Donald Knowles, seems loose and meandering, and shows no signs of the taut economy of

Willeford's prose. My guess is that these chapters are Sanders' work.

On his first day back in harness, simmering under the heat and humiliation of his demotion, Brown loses his temper with an arrogant motorist and smashes him in the face. "He shouldn't have smiled," says Brown.

> Bones and flesh gave with a sickening crunch and blood spurted from his face. His grin disappeared—and I knew my job with the Los Angeles Police Department went with it. Also my chances for remaining both at large and in L.A. . . . I think that's where my headache began.

Believing that he's just committed murder, Brown leaves the scene and hops a bus just as far as his money will take him: Dallas, Texas. But quicker than you can drawl "Hail to the thief," Brown gets mixed up with a bunch of crazed Okie kidnappers and a "she-devil" with a bullwhip. As in so many other Willeford novels, the protagonist is a picaresque rascal who gets himself into a world-sized meatgrinder of trouble, but somehow manages to wriggle out of it, not too much the worse for wear, shrugging it off with little more than a hot shower and a stiff drink, and if you're looking for a moral . . . don't.

As soon as I could find him again, I told Dennis about my discovery and gave him one of several copies I'd recently acquired, never paying more than five bucks for any of them. Next I told a couple of other paperback junkies—Lynn Munroe, who announced the news in his collectible paperback catalogue and a vintage paperback publication called *Books Are Everything*, and Gary Lovisi, maverick crime fiction publisher who blurbed it in his own magazine for biblio-maniacs, *Paperback Parade*. The price of this previously cheap paperback original immediately skyrocketed. Within a year I was seeing *The Whip Hand* going for $200, then $300, and then I quit looking. I used to drive cars that cost me $300.

And what about the differences between this book and the Gold Medal version? My advice would be to save your money and spend it on a couple of extra copies of this one to give to your friends or squirrel away in your collection. By and large, they're extremely minor. Name changes. A line here and there. The biggest change I can think of is the introduction. The Gold Medal version has five extra pages tacked on, detailing Bill Brown's downfall from the Auto Theft Bureau. *This* draft, which I'm betting is pure or almost pure Willeford, is succinct and hard-boiled. *This* set-up, plus the apparently-fatal punch, takes all of 340 words. A couple of paragraphs later and Bill Brown is on the lam. That isn't just hard-boiled, it's great writing. It reminds me of the way Robert Mitchum's character sums up his back story in *Macao:* "A hassle with a redhead."

My guess is that some meddlesome editor at Fawcett Gold Medal was trying to earn his pay by "improving" the manuscript. Or, after hanging onto his copy of the manuscript for several years, Sanders kept fussing with it, then tried Gold Medal again, thinking he'd improved it so much that Willeford was no longer entitled to credit, and got it published. *¿Quién sabe?*

We made a few attempts to locate W. Franklin Sanders, without success. Apparently Sanders wrote no other books, at least under that name. And although Willeford was a notorious practical joker and prankster, I came to realize that Sanders was in fact a real person, not a mere literary device.

There was a letter from Sanders to Willeford found along with the mss. of *Deliver Me from Dallas!* in the bottom of a box of other mss. and correspondence, when Don Herron and Dennis McMillan went through his literary papers shortly after his death. The letter is interesting in several respects, the most striking being its tone of shared camaraderie, the unstated facts about their relationship, the apparent mutual qualities of their lives. It also establishes certain facts about when and where *Deliver Me From Dallas!* was probably written, despite the fact that no year is specified in the heading.

85 Poplar
Ross
11 June

Dear Chas:

I left your last letter to home this morn, but will drop a note to say the book is being mailed this morning before twelve, high noon. I made the changes from "motor" to "engine" and changed the "mouse" to "I was quiet as the settling dust." The typewriter had been returned in order to halt the rental charges, so I made these corrections neatly, with a pen. I don't know how that mouse got in right there! I agree it had to go, but I didn't want to add too much and mess up the page badly, so I used the comparatively short "settling dust" in its place.

Say—I was wondering, aren't you well-acquainted with a book reviewer on the SB paper? Maybe he'd read our masterpiece and write a nice column on being honored for the first time by being allowed to review a book pre-publication. Ha!

Will answer your letter more completely tomorrow after a careful perusal.

How about the coincidence of my asking you when you and Mary Jo were gettin' hitched and your letter crossing in the mail to verify my hunch? I think you'll be very happy— much happier than in other circumstances which there is no need to delve into here. I also think it a smart, intelligent move on your part, and can see no reason why you should look further for a wonderful companion to grow old with. Keep me posted on the romantic progress.

x

I hope Jim Bishop will give us a quick (comparatively) report. Like you, I can use the money.

12 Jun

Having had the afternoon off yesterday, I went in to San Rafael about 10 A.M. and put the book on its merry way, proceeded to get wall-eyed, and am a number one candidate for another divorce this morning. Oh, well, you'll add to the ranks and I'll drop out—it all goes in accordance with Emerson's essay on Compensation—balances out one for one, one in, one out. I can write more as a single man, anyhow, and I can't make a woman stay happy. It's like Grace said last night—I just build her up and soften her up, then boom! down goes spaghetti. Is there an 'h' in spaget? I'm going down to the orderly room this morning and see if I can get on a shipment going somewhere—anywhere. I've been still too, too long.

Ran into Okey up town and we had a couple together— that's what started all my trouble. I yust kept going and going, and it culminated in a very bitter display last night at home. Woe is me. This time I think she means it. Okey said to tell you hello and to do something obscene—I forget just what it was.

Maybe I can go to ADC or CDC or someplace. Thought sure I'd hear from my attaché application before this. Never come at a propitious time, do they? Always when you don't want it.

The express man told me the book would be in New York within a week. We should hear one way or the other by Aug 1, don't you think?

I'm a shade disgruntled for this job of correspondence to flow smoothly, so I better let it went as is.

 Hasta luego, amigo mio,

Sandie

The chronology of Willeford's military service has confused many a writer, this one included. However, Betsy Willeford recently provided me with the dates of his enlistments and her own annotations, which clear things up considerably. After Willeford was discharged from the army in July 1949, he enlisted in the United States Air Force in November 1949 (Willeford had served in the Army Air Corps during his very first enlistment which began in 1935, when he was sixteen and lied about his age in order to be accepted–the USAF was created as a separate service in 1947). During the 1949 interval he gave his permanent mailing address as General Delivery, Dallas, Texas, even though for most of that time he was studying art and art history at Universitarias de Belles Artes in Lima, Peru, only to be "rusticated" as Betsy says, "when university officials learned he had no under-graduate degree and no high school diploma." Between March 22, 1950 and November 21, 1951 he was assigned to Hamilton Air Force Base, near Novato, California, with liaison duty from Hamilton through April 1952.

This explains the Ross address on the Sanders letter. Ross is in the Novato area. Willeford met Sanders at Marin Community College, says Betsy, and met future wife Mary Jo when he went in to pay a parking ticket in Santa Barbara, where he was temporarily assigned as a recruiting sergeant. This also explains Willeford's being "well-acquainted with a book reviewer on the SB paper." ADC stands for Air Defense Command, but I haven't been able to find out what CDC stands for. Jim Bishop's identity is also still a mystery, as is "Okey's."

And so, my theory is that *Deliver Me From Dallas!* was written during 1950-51. According to Betsy Willeford, that "almost has to be correct." During this period Willeford used to drive down to San Francisco on weekends and check into the Powell

Hotel to write. He was already a published writer. His work had been included in the Outcast Poets series issued by New York's Alicat Bookshop in 1947, and *Proletarian Laughter*, a chapbook collection of poems and seven prose "schematics" about the war was issued by Alicat in 1948. Willeford's first book-length publication was *High Priest of California*, his first novel, published by Royal Books in 1953. A little over thirty years and a dozen or so novels later (depending on how you count them), *Miami Blues* made him a star. Four years later Willeford died of heart failure at age 69.

Willeford's belated success with the Hoke Moseley series also spawned the now thriving sub-genre of South Florida crime fiction. But Willeford was so much more than a great American crime writer. Take away the word "crime" and you're getting warm. Great American writer, period.

In 1997 McMillan published *Willeford*, a rambling biography of sorts by Don Herron, who became acquainted with Charles Willeford after Willeford showed up one day for Herron's Dashiell Hammett Tour of San Francisco. Herron had never heard of the writer before, but he quickly made up for lost time. The time he spent with Willeford, hanging out and corresponding with him, was fruitful enough to fill a 470-page book, complete with an extensive bibliography and lots of great photos (no index, though), which is usually, except when Herron spends way too much time talking about himself, extremely entertaining and fairly enlightening about our hero. One of the things I've loved the most about Willeford's style of writing, with its seductively simple prose and poker-faced humor, is that I've felt that I could hear Willeford *telling* each story himself. I could feel his presence, hear his voice. One of the best things about Herron's book is that he helps recreate Willeford's presence. Herron recounts several anecdotes about Willeford's penchant for jokes and pranks. "He's kidding when he's not kidding," quipped James Crumley, after eating lunch with Willeford, Les Standiford, Jim Hall, and Dennis McMillan at an Irish bar called Duffy's in Coral Gables.

It seems a fair bet that Willeford, who was also known for his love of titles with double meanings, probably was writing down his "General Delivery, Dallas, Texas" address one day when he thought of the title for this book.

By the time I made my discovery, Charles Willeford had been dead for three years. Willeford, his widow Betsy, Dennis McMillan–nobody knew that *Deliver Me From Dallas!* had been published by Fawcett Gold Medal. The Fawcett connection (excuse the pun) is probably one of the best jokes of all. Knox Burger, editor at Gold Medal in the Fifties, would later appreciate Willeford's writing, but at the time he was no fan. In a note to Willeford's agent, Burger said: "I don't like this guy Willeford's hero. I don't like this guy Willeford's novel. In fact, I don't like this guy Willeford! Don't send me anymore [sic] of his books!" Many years later, when McMillan asked Willeford about Burger's rejection letter, he laughed and said, "He confused *me* with my *characters,* you see."

Somewhere, Charles Willeford, that old joker, is having a good, long laugh about our confusion over the curious circumstances of this book. Although I never met him, I can imagine him looking at us with a sly, enigmatic smile, and saying: "I think you'll find it an 'interesting' read. . . ."

DELIVER ME FROM DALLAS

Chapter One

BILL BROWN

THIS FIRST DAY BACK IN HARNESS WAS far from pleasant after spending three soft years in the Auto Theft Bureau. Unpleasant but logical. It was all very clear. You got caught with your hand out, they lower the boom, and you find yourself in my spot. Back in uniform. Turning with the signals at Eighth and Broadway, downtown L.A.

I'd forgotten what being a traffic cop was like but I was remembering now. Fast.

The day was a scorcher and the people were mad. I had my hands full, keeping pedestrians from jumping under wheels and drivers from throwing cars over pedestrians. Life was cheap on that corner.

My pants were too tight. Holdovers from beat-walking days, they wouldn't adjust to the bulge–the one I had put on doing the sedentary, paper-shuffling work in the Bureau. The big .45 now replacing the compact job I'd carried in the old shoulder holster wasn't improving the kidney department.

The kidneys hurt. My feet hurt. I was hot. And I was sore.

A driver started to cut right, against the red. I blasted with the whistle in time to prevent plural manslaughter. He stopped, and when I turned my back on him I was grinding my teeth. I remembered something I could yell at him without breaking too many regulations and turned back–just in time. He was making the turn anyhow.

1

He heard the whistle–I guess they heard it in Pomona–and stopped again.

Then he grinned. He shouldn't have grinned.

I was very deliberate about the thing. I walked over to his car, opened the door, and smashed my fist, loaded with everything I hated about this corner, into his silly grinning face. Bones and flesh gave with a sickening crunch and blood spurted from his face. His grin disappeared–and I knew my job with the Los Angeles Police Department went with it. Also my chances for remaining both at large and in L.A., with this final topper added to my recent sins. I think that's where my headache began.

I'd never had a headache in my life, but before I walked away from that scene the one I had felt like it had been there forever. It was like two barbed arrows running through my temples and gleefully entwining where they had no business meeting.

I forced myself to think–fast. A kid about seventeen was standing next to me with his jaw at half-mast.

"You sure did hit him!"

"Never mind. Can you drive a car?"

"Show me one I can't drive!"

"Know where Georgia Street Receiving is?"

"Sure, I know."

"Get going!"

The kid was quick-witted. He pushed the sleeping victim over in the seat, climbed in beside the body, and shot away down Eighth toward Figueroa. If his speed in getting away from that corner held out to Georgia Street it might give the man a chance, in case it wasn't too late when he started. I admired the boy's skill, but the last glimpse I had of the limbernecked passenger through the window gave me a sleazy feeling.

2

I spent a couple of minutes getting the crowd moving. There was no more blood for them to see, so they weren't too hard to get going. When the confusion was normal again I took a long breath and a quick look around the intersection.

I walked away, looking straight ahead, letting the blaring horns, the fist-shaking pedestrians and the signals work out their own solutions. I had problems of my own.

I cut over to Main and walked into the Bus Station. Of course I had to be acquainted with the cop on duty in there. It was Griego of the Main Street Detail, and he was hoping the other Mexican he was watching would make a wrong move. He bobbed his head in recognition.

"Bill Brown. I heard you were back in harness."

"Griego," I said, "you haven't seen me. Okay?"

"Sure, Bill. In trouble again?"

"You haven't seen me."

"I haven't seen you." He shifted his interest back to the Mexican. I found a vacant phone booth and dialed my apartment. I was in luck—the brother answered. I tried to shake some of the pain out of my head so I could remember what I'd need.

"Ed. I want you to come down to the Bus Station on Main."

"I go on duty in a hour, Bill."

"Never mind. Bring me a suit, shirt and a hat."

"What for? Why not come home and change clothes?"

"Tell you when you got here. I'll be in the men's can."

"It'll be a few minutes, Bill." He hung up.

I went to the men's room and bought a shine, to pass the time while I worried about when the alarm would go out for me. A cop can do a lot of things in L.A.

He can keep girls on the side, accept bribes and gifts, and sometimes he can get away with a quiet little shakedown. One thing he can not do. He can't hit a citizen on a busy corner on a hot day. Citizens pay taxes. And besides, I had hit this one too hard. Much too hard. I paid the Negro boy for the shine and eased out into the waiting room.

When I couldn't put it off any longer, I checked my billfold. I'd had it figured. Short. Much too short. I read the signs ringed around the ceiling which showed the fares to various points: L. A. to Frisco. L. A. to Seattle. L.A. to Chicago. L.A. to Dallas. Dallas caught my eye because it fit.

It was the farthest point my billfold would cover. I wasn't known in Dallas. It was big, I'd heard, and I didn't want to drop into some wide place in the road. So, Dallas it was.

I didn't think it would be intelligent for a uniformed cop to walk up to a ticket window and buy a ticket to Dallas, and have to answer the old question of all ticket clerks, "One way, Sir?", so I went back to the can again.

"Shine, go buy a one-way ticket to Dallas for me." I pressed the exact fare into his hand. He was surprised but he went.

He was back in no time. I took the ticket and handed him a dime. He stared at the dime awhile, but when it didn't grow he finally put it away.

The brother, Ed, came in. He hadn't thought to use a suitcase, for some unknown reason, and the clothes were bundled up in a newspaper. I took the bundle, squandered a nickel and entered a pay toilet to change. I could hear the brother walking around nervously on the hollow-sounding tile. I swore at him under my breath. He'd brought the suit I hated most, the green gabardine, and with it a yellow sportshirt and a checkered cap. A blind man could identify me at a hundred yards if they ever learned what garb I was traveling in! The kid had the taste of a Boyle Heights Vaselino. I let him sweat his curiosity till I finished changing.

"What's up, Bill?"

No one was in earshot.

4

"I hit a guy."

Ed shook his head sadly.

"Yeah. A citizen–and I think I hit him too hard. I'm going to Dallas. If I can get there in this outfit. . . ."

"I was in a hurry. You said–"

"Yeah, I know. I'll try to let you know what the scoop is when I get set."

"It'll blow over, Bill–why don't you stick around?"

"No. I just got out of one jam. They'll play rough this time."

"How about the apartment, Bill? It costs too much for me by myself."

"That reminds me. How much dough you got?"

"Only a buck."

"Give it here." He did. "Move one of your girls in. They all got jobs. Or sell my gun to tide you over."

"No. I want that gun. Don't worry, I'll manage. Just take care of yourself."

We shook hands. He used the same newspaper and wrapped up the uniform, belt, harness, sap and handcuffs. I poked him in the ribs as he walked out. I didn't think I'd ever see him again. A good kid. Not overly sharp maybe, but a damn good cop. My headache was worse, if possible.

I hated to spend any dough. I was going to need every nickel–twice. But I couldn't stand it any longer. I bought a small tin of aspirin at the drug counter and washed down the first four at the fountain with a coke. I sat there expectantly, with my teeth hard together. No effect. I waited a little longer and became convinced this was some special kind of headache. I hadn't taken enough. I asked for a glass of water and took four more, and dug for the change to buy two more boxes for the bus ride.

I was really sweating out the time. Things had worked okay so far but I had a feeling time and luck were both reaching

5

hard ground. I could still see Griego, and he was still not seeing me. I know he had seen Ed, but he wouldn't spill. We had worked together once and he had swiped a double-handful of wristwatches when we reported to the scene of a jewelry store burglary. Sometimes it pays to have something on a friend.

I counted my cash. It was easy. One buck and one half. I'd be hungry when we rolled into Dallas. I checked the clock. Almost time, and I edged toward the gates. I had the fidgets; was watching one entrance, then another. A glimpse in a glass gave me a shudder. I peeled off the checkered cap and threw it in a waste basket.

The call finally came. El Centro, Yuma, Phoenix, Douglas, Lordsburg, El Paso, Fort Worth . . . and Dallas. That was me.

First in line, I grabbed a seat in the rear by the window. The bus soon filled, and the driver pulled out into the traffic stream. We passed the front of the station and I saw two men from the Central Station talking to Griego. I watched, keeping my head in shadow. He was shaking his head. Griego, I love you!

Through the city, over the L.A. river bridge and out past Lincoln Park. Onto the highway stretching through the orange groves, Arizona, New Mexico, Texas, Dallas, Freedom. . . . It looked like I had made it.

Chapter Two

JUNIOR KNOWLES

The kid wasn't bawlin' no more. She was quiet, 'cept for once't in a while a shaky sniffle–like she'd like to cry some more. I waited. She was starin' at the floor an' it was plain as day she was a-wantin' to watch me but was scairt to look.

When she sniffled her mouth would shimmy like a fishin' cork with a perch too lil' to git caught a-tryin' to tug the worm off'n the hook. Rest o' the time she jes' set an' stared. An' ever lil' bit tears would squeeze outta the corners of her eyes an' roll acrost the red marks on the sides of her face. I'd back-an'-forthed her a few times with my hand to stop the bawlin' in the first place. Sorta practicin' for when me an' Leonie'd git married an' have kids.

Leonie, she likes kids an' wants to have some. Up 'til now it'd been mostly talk 'twixt us, 'cause where could I make the money we woulda needed? But today things was a lot different an' I was thinkin' how Leonie's eyes would pop out when I told her.

This here husky kid settin' there in that old straight chair a-gawkin' at the floor wouldn't never need nothin'. Nothin' money could git, leastways. I'd been a-hopin' she'd squall ag'in. I hated to lay it onto her 'thout no reason. Donald an' El was squirmy that first time I'd shut her up. I twisted around facin' the table they was settin' at, lil' rustle sounds slippin' back an' forth around 'am.

They was countin' the money ag'in.

Donald, he was smilin' like the time me an' Paw chipped in to git them mail-order pants an' galluses for him. Shakin' his head side to side, dreamy-like.

I don't reckon he was really countin'–jes' feelin' an' sortin' an' day-dreamin'.

With old El it was different. He was countin'. The careful an' quick-like way of a man behind the bars in a bank. So dead set on it I woulda laughed, but . . . fifteen thousand dollars!

I couldn't hardly believe it myself. Shoulda been easy, what with the way I'd figgered out the whole plan. It shore had worked smooth– jes' like a fresh-oiled pulley inside a wall-rope.

Splittin' three ways, we had us the same as five thousand silver dollars apiece! Me, my brother an' old El Mercer! None of us hadn't never had nothin'. An' if we'd a-stayed in Oklahoma 'stead of comin' on this trip I'd thought up we never woulda had nothin'. But now–we was rich!

'Course, I'd planned this trip for money-makin' from the beginnin'. But ridin' down here to Dallas in El's old LaSalle I didn't have no idy of makin' this much. Reckon that fancy-pants feller from Tulsa that come inta the pool hall to wait while the garage fixed his car was the thing that changed my luck. Guess he knows how to play eight-ball-in-the-side now. I had to shoot awful bad to keep from beatin' him so bad he woulda quit.

I had fifty dollars whenever he did quit. I got El an' Donald talked into comin' down here and tyin' the fifty dollars up in a load of whiskey. That was more money than I'd saw in a coon's age, an' I knowed I could double it or triple it, maybe,

8

takin' the whiskey acrost to Oklahoma an' sellin' it to them college boys in Norman. But in Dallas things never worked out like that.

We got here 'thout no trouble. But them signs all along beside the road in Texas a-tellin' how the state fair was on in Dallas had dern near drove my brother Donald crazy. He's about a man's age, but you'da thought he was a half-growed kid the way he wanted to git out to them fairgrounds so bad. I felt sorry for Donald an' I hadn't never seen a fair big as this one neither, so I give in an' made El foller the signs to the fairgrounds an' we went in to jes' look around a lil' bit.

For a while we walked up an' down lookin' at ever'thing on the midway. I wouldn't give Donald no money to ride no rides like he worried me for, till we come acrost the shootin' gallery with them fancy twenty-two's. Iff'n I spent money to shoot I'd hafta let Donald ride, dead certain. There's jes' somethin' inside o' me that any kinda gun gives the itch. Seems like first thing I knowed we was about out of money.

I still don't see how we spent so much, but it shore hadn't took long. El kept a-tellin' me I was spendin' too much but I told him to shut up, whose money was it. He whined at me.

"Awright, Junior. Jus' don't fergit, you done the spendin'. Ten dollars ain't hardly more'n enough to buy gas an' oil to git home, let alone whiskey to haul to Norman."

"Looky here, El, I don't wanta hear no more about what we spent. Come right down to it some of that there money was spent on you. So shet up!"

El was took care of with that but I never felt no better. Never kept what he said from bein' true jes' 'cause I wouldn't let him say it no more. Wasn't like me, to git suckered outta the money I'd meant to be a starter for me an' Leonie to git hitched. No use a-cryin' over it—we might as well find Donald an' git rollin', I figgered. I seen him down the midway a piece.

He was squattin' down a-talkin' to a li'l gal that musta been about six year old. She was dressed up all in red an' was cute as anything. Me an' El walked down there.

"Junior," Donald said, "gimmie a dime. I wanta buy this little gal a ice cream cone."

"No." I told him. "We done spent all we're a-goin' to. Let's go."

"Aw, Junior, just a dime. Ain't she a sweet little ol' gal?"

"Donald, we got to git movin'! Turn 'at kid's hand aloose an' let her git."

He seen I was mad and let go of her. I give her a scary look, but she never got scairt. She taken a step tords Donald an' opened the top of the li'l red purse she was a-holdin' on to. "I got money," she told Donald. "See?"

I went over quick an' looked, an' old El was right behind me. Doggoned if that purse wasn't plumb loaded with nickels an' dimes. Old El slobbered some an' reached in front o' me for the purse.

"Lemma count it for you, little girl," he said through his fat, ugly grin.

I caught El's wrist, squeezed, an' taken the purse myself.

"I'll count it, El."

I made out like I was countin' the money but I was reely doin' some fast thinkin'. The li'l yeller-headed kid had put one hand back into Donald's, a-lookin' up at him like she done had her ice cream an' he was it.

"Three eighty-five," I told El, but there was prob'ly more'n that.

I handed Donald a dime an' dropped the rest in my pocket. El watched it slide outta my hand like a hongry dog watchin' a man eatin' a rare steak.

"Buy her some ice cream, Donald, an' see you don't let her outta sight."

She looked happy walkin' away with him. I tried to watch ever'body an' see iff'n anybody cared about her a-wanderin' off with Donald. Didn't look like nobody give a hoot. Didn't make sense.

El commenced whinin' about that three eighty-five.

"Shet up, El–I'm a-thinkin'."

That li'l gal musta got lost or she wouldn't be in that crowd 'thout none of her folks bein' around. Iff'n she was lost her folks was shore to be huntin' her. Wasn't hard to tell she b'longed to folks with money. I never had no money an' I was gonna hafta git some. Iff'n she was lost for a spell an' her folks had money they'd pay a reward. Iff'n we could take her home we'd git that reward.

I was prob'ly the only human bein' at the fairgrounds that knowed who she was an' where she lived. I don't never miss much, an' that white strip of cloth sewed inside her purse had told that. The purse was stuck inside my shirt now.

The quicker her kin found the kid the less they'd worry. Less they'd pay, too. I could jes keep her with us a day or so first an' they'd pay a sight more. I could feel my heart beatin' faster when the plan come to me.

We never had no place to keep her, but I figgered iff'n her Paw *thought* we was gonna keep her we could git the same amount in one day–by jes tellin' him how much we needed. Iff'n he was bullheaded we'd send him a piece of one of her ears, sliced off. That'd prob'ly fix it so's he'd pay. It was so simple I had to grin. As simple as I seen it in all the pitcher shows, only this was the first time I'd fell inta the chance to work it.

Donald would do whatever I said an' I knowed I could bluff El to do it. That or it wouldn't be healthy for El. We'd only git this one chance't an' nobody was gonna keep me from a-takin' it.

"El, that li'l gal means five thousand dollars apiece to us," I told him—slow-like so's maybe it'd sink in.

"What's 'at?"

"I said how'd you like to leave Dallas with five thousand dollars in yore jeans—all in bran' new tens, twen'ies an' fives?"

"Junior, doggone you, yer tryin' to git me in trouble." His lips was fluttery.

"Naw, El. Not trouble. Jes' some reward money. Couldn't hardly git in no trouble a-takin' that li'l gal back to her Paw, could we?"

"Ner git five thousand dollars, neither."

"We could by keepin' her a few days first."

"Where in thunder could we keep her? Junior, I gotta good idee these here Texans don't fret none too much 'bout how they treat kidnappers. We best don't talk no more about it."

"You scairt, El?"

"Shore I'm scairt! Ain't you?"

"Naw. Not for five thousand dollars—cash—apiece. . . ."

"Apiece?" El licked his lips an' his eyes was makin' jumpy li'l wiggles.

"Shore, apiece. Lookit how she's dressed. An' carryin' that handful o' change around an' her jes' a shaver of a gal. That much reward would be easy!"

"An' if we git caught?"

"How? Who knows we come to Dallas? This here's a city, man; it ain't knowed as Big D for nothin'. Nobody here known us neither . . . call Donald."

El called my brother, jes' like I knowed he would.

The rest wasn't hard a-tall. We jes' hadta be sorta careful, that's all. I never told Donald no whole lot. Knowed I could tell him as we went along, a smidgin at a time. The li'l gal never put up no fuss. Reckon that was 'cause she'd took to Donald so. He had her a-callin' him Unca Don' awready.

We went out on the Fort Worth road a piece an' drove in at a cheap-lookin' tourist camp. We was low on money till we could collect the reward, an' them tourist camps don't trust nothin' but cash on the bar'lhead. The kid thought it was a funny game when I hid her under the big towsack down on the floor of the car. Nobody seen she was with us.

Soon's we was in the cabin I paid for, I yanked the piece of cloth with the kid's name on it outta the purse I'd kept. When I wrote the note I printed it with my left hand so's to be shore it couldn't be brung home to me. I told El jes' how to take the note and the scrap from the purse to the house at the address it showed, an' told him to shove it under the front door. He was gone for quite a spell an' I begin to worry before he come back an' said he'd did jes' like I said an' never had no trouble.

I left El at the cabin to watch after the li'l gal while me an' Donald went to watch for the reward to be brung out. I located a good spot to stop an' watch from, 'bout a quarter-mile from the place I'd spoke of in the note. It was s'prisin' how short a spell we hadta wait.

A big shiny car stopped acrost from the fence around that big cement fact'ry an' somebody throwed somethin' out in the ditch an' started right off tords town ag'in. I waited at least a half a hour to be shore nobody was follerin' that car when it come out or watchin' that spot. The road was jes' about plumb quiet when I couldn't hold in no longer. I hadta know.

I stopped the old LaSalle about fifty yards away with the engine runnin' an' sent Donald over to git the bundle outta the ditch. He was right back in a few minutes but it seemed like a long time. He was a-totin' a big leather suitcase, an' iff'n my plan had worked it'd be stuffed with fifteen thousand

13

dollars! My fingers was a-tremblin' so much I couldn't hardly git it open.

Reckon I never had no call to be worried. The money was in there, awright, in li'l bundles with strips o' paper around ever one tellin' how much. Reckon they ain't a city-slicker a-livin' that'd try to trick me after that note I wrote—he knowed I wasn't joshin'. Leastways 'til he knowed his gal was gonna be safe, an' he never knowed it. He paid off like a Number One oil well on the Cherokee reservation.

It'd been real easy—an' I never stayed only long enough to make shore it was money. I whupped the old car around an' drove the two-three miles back to the tourist camp.

An' here we was the nex' mornin'—a mite sleepy 'cause we'd been up mosta the night a-countin' money. It was all there. All we had to do now was kill the li'l gal an' be gone. Only El an' Donald never knowed about this last smart part o' my plannin'. I was jes' fixin' to spring it on 'em.

I was beginnin' to like Dallas an' I'd settled on stayin' there to live a spell. I wanted to git some soft livin' for a while. Tall buildin's. Paved roads, Leonie an' good livin'! I'd had enough hell, hard work an' pore folks around me to last till doom's day awready.

Nobody nor nothin' wasn't gonna stop me. Not Donald. Not El. An' not killin' that kid, neither. The hard times'd be made up for now. I ain't never seen a purtier sight than them three big piles of money a-layin' on the table.

One of 'em was mine. El an' Donald was both so happy it looked as if they was tryin' to outshine each other. They hadn't never been that happy before.

I wondered iff'n I oughtta make one of them kill the li'l gal. Draw straws maybe. But I decided ag'in it. Woulda been a awful smart way to make shore El never spilt the beans to make him do it. 'Fore he had the money I coulda made him,

14

easy, but now I was kinda doubtful. I coulda bossed Donald into it too but I didn't figger it'd be fair, him so young. Reckon that brought it right back to what I was a-wantin'. Left it all up to me. Gittin' her past talkin' or recognizin' me might save my gullet from gittin' overstretched at the end of a Texas rope.

"Donald. Take her into the bathroom."

He done what I said, jes' like always, an' shet the door on the way back out.

"El," I said. "This here is where we come to the partin' of the ways. We gotta make a clean gitaway an' to do that we gotta watch out. Me an' Donald will keep yore ol' car, but we'll drive you downtown to the bus station. That there car's gonna hafta be ditched purty soon, so ain't no use o' you takin' it. You wanta go back to Oklahoma, don'tcha?"

"Where else would I go but to Oklahoma?"

"Nowheres. Donald an' me, we're goin' to Noo Orleens."

"What we gonna do in Noo Orleens, Junior? I wanta go back to Oklahoma, too."

"Naw. Me an' you are gonna split up too. You're goin' by train an' I'll drive the car an' meetcha there."

"But Junior. . . ."

"The only way is to travel in ones. I seen it too many times."

"Heck—I wanta buy some new clo'es, an' maybe a car . . . an' we can git drunk as seven hunderd dollars an'. . . ."

"Hold yore hosses, Donald! We'll pick us out some new clo'es 'fore we leave, awright. But then we'll split up an' travel like I toldja. An' that's that. Ever'thing also is gonna hafta wait."

"What about that little gal?" El ast me.

"I'm a-tyin' her up an' a-leavin' her here. They'll find her. You take the suitcase, El, an' carry yore part in it. It'll make you more like a bus rider. Donald, put ours in one o' them

15

towsacks in the car. We'll git some grips when we git the clo'es."

They got real busy. El was glad to git the suitcase an' I was honin' to git rid of him soon as possible. I wanted him to be long gone when it come out about the kid bein' found dead.

El picked up the suitcase an' stumbled outside an' clumb inta the car. Donald was jes' standin' there with our money in the towsack.

"Go ahead an' git in the car, Donald. I'm gonna tie the li'l gal up. I'll be right out."

Donald never wanted to see me tie her up 'cause he liked her so much. He looked sorta sad as he walked out an' shet the door. I felt some better 'bout not tellin' him an' El my real plan.

I went straight off to the bathroom. She tried to back through the far wall to git away from me. She wanted to cry but I reckon she remembered what happened last time she raised a ruckus – I'm purty strong.

It wasn't no worse than wringin' a chicken's neck.

I sorta folded her up an' stuck her in the closet for towels an' such. Then I went out an' locked the door an' felt mighty good walkin' over to the car.

Donald an' El was used to me doin' the leadin' an' had left me the driver seat. As we rolled past the office of the camp I throwed the key so's it'd fall under the light a-stickin' out over the front porch.

Then I swung her over onto the highway an' headed tords Dallas.

CHAPTER THREE

Bill Brown

It was rather warm in Dallas. Carrying the coat-part of my present wardrobe, I stepped from the bus and dripped my way into the station—trying to strain some air into my lungs from the hanging mass of motionless humidity.

The end of the line. The middle of the United States. Dallas: A gathered-in collection of white buildings trying to be a city. Canyons between the buildings forming flues for the torridity bouncing off pavement and bricks. Sprawling and shimmering in the inexhaustible fires of a Texas sun.

I'd been thinking about a lot of things through the thousand deserts we crossed on the miserable trip from L.A. I had chosen a good place to start over.

The dubious prospect of this starting over was crowding for space with the pain in my head.

My assets were in great shape. As an ex-cop I could hardly apply for police work with the thing in L.A. hanging fire. A green gabardine with black shoes! I'd look good to prospective employers in that get-up. A three-day growth of black beard and no razor. One thin dime in the cash on hand account. Ten cents. I could at least buy coffee.

Then my eyes fell upon the row of coin-operated parcel lockers against the wall. Looking at them and fingering the

17

lonesome dime in my pocket reminded me of the ancient key-switch con. Why not? With a suitcase I could check into a hotel on my looks. With the added tempting possibility that there would be a razor and maybe a change of socks in said suitcase—if I were lucky enough to meet a character innocent enough to fall for the old sleight of hand game. The socks I had on were getting squishy from the perspiration running into my shoes—I think that's what made up my mind to try it. You might call it a case of necessity being the mother of intention.

I dropped the cash asset into a slot, and palmed the locker key. All I had to do was wait for a sucker. One who would relinquish his suitcase to a rough-looking stranger. The idea that I could easily starve to death before finding one that stupid had me a bit worried.

But I didn't even have time for a mental rehearsal before I saw this man of the soil come in the main entrance and plod flat-footedly in my direction. A loose-looking, ultra-seedy hick. Faded Levi's hugging sockless ankles and a coat over his once-white undershirt. Hot as it was, the coat must have been his personal concession to the conventional. His sweaty face had been weathered into crevices starting from four directions of the compass and running carefree through the fat toward the corners of his mouth. He wasn't pretty.

But the all-leather two-suiter bag he was carrying was, in my hungry eyes, a beautiful creation. I concentrated on it. But taking it was harder than I expected after psychoanalyzing him on his trek across the waiting room. For a minute I thought he wasn't going to let go of it.

"I just want to check it for you, sir." He nearly sprawled on the floor from the violent jerk I had to use to get the bag. While he recovered I shoved it into an empty locker and met him next with an out-stretched hand.

"A dime. It takes dimes."

The farmer handed me one, with his baleful yellow eyes looking into mine. I put the dime into the slot, exchanged keys with him–giving him the dud, of course–and held out my hand again. He studied it and finally, reluctantly, placed a nickel in my palm.

"Thank you, sir. God bless you," I said, pretending to move away.

He carefully pocketed what he thought was his key, muttered something about letting beggars into the bus station, and made for the lunchroom. As the door to the lunchroom closed, the door to the locker opened. Thirty seconds later I was outside on the street with a suitcase. And my headache. And near prostration from the heat.

But hot as it was I covered two blocks in a hurry and checked into the Southwesterner Hotel. In my relief at being able to set up temporary comfortable headquarters, I unconsciously became an honest man. I registered as Bill Brown, Los Angeles. I guess it was just as well–the clerk looked at me like it was a phony name, just like they always do. The bellboy tried to take my bag but I was too quick for him. I couldn't afford the price of a tip, and that way I'd earn a little less contempt. I don't appreciate contempt.

"I can manage it."

He looked disappointed for a second but led me to the elevator and pushed the button for the fifth floor. He hadn't entirely written me off as a prospect.

"Anything you needs, Boss?"

"No."

"Ah means *any*thing." And he grinned, displaying a set of golden choppers.

"The way you say 'anything' sounds like you mean it."

"Mean it? Boss, jus' you give me one reques'."

19

I guess he did mean it, but I couldn't have cared less. I opened the door to 502; then the window. I turned the cold water on in the shower, undressed, came back to the bed, and opened my new bag.

There was nothing in it but money.

Fives—tens—and these, a little digging showed, had been put on top to hide the twenties! Stunned, I started to count, and then said the hell with it. I found the phone and called the desk for a fifth of I. W. Harper and a razor. I closed the bag and pushed it under the bed.

The shower felt good. I felt good even with a splitting headache. And I was a very fortunate ex-cop. I didn't care how the hick got it. Or how he felt. All I knew was that he wasn't getting it back. With possible manslaughter charges haunting me, a little robbery without firearms on the side would just be the spice of variety.

A knock on the door brought the bellboy with the fifth and a razor. That Negro had a sixth sense, or powerful logic, for he'd added shaving cream and a toothbrush to my order on his own. I gave him a twenty bonus.

His eyes showed me about ten dollars worth of whites, but the real profit showed through the big grin he turned on. All the gold that wasn't in Fort Knox was shining in his face.

"Hot damn! Ah sho' does thank you, suh!"

I waved him out magnanimously, wondering why I should be anything but generous. Easy come. . . .

I poured a triple from the fifth, and when it found the shrunken boundaries of my stomach I knew I'd better eat—with priority. I dressed and then fattened my empty wallet with a nice sheaf of twenties. I delayed my own appetite and counted the money, being curious to know just how affluent I had become.

Forty-seven hundred hard ones passed through my fingertips. Some better than the razor and change of socks I had expected, and very nice odds for a dime!

I couldn't really hide the bag, so I stowed it in the closet, caught the elevator down and made my way to the grill next door to my new home. I took plenty of time over a medium-rare sirloin, getting the most out of each mouthful of juicy Texas steer. Very satisfying to the inner man and very helpful in giving my mind time to do a little cog work.

Taxi to a quiet section of town and a room in a boarding house. Hole up incognito for a couple of weeks. That would be the smart thing. That would give the hick enough time to get discouraged and hitchhike to whatever destination he had in mind. And I could contact Ed from there if I couldn't learn what I wanted to know from the papers.

After a brief retirement I could look around. I'd pick and choose. Find the sort of job I pleased and become a respectable citizen of Dallas. Summer couldn't last forever. By the time I followed the steak with apple pie a la mode, I had settled on that plan.

I hauled the overload out of the chair and moved over to the cashier's booth.

"What have you got for a headache?"

Hollywood thinks *its* girls have glamour. Nuts. She gave me some powders, wrapped in blue oil paper.

"Just open one and shake it down your throat."

I did just that, but I didn't notice any relief. I was beginning to think I might invest my wealth in an effective headache potion of some kind. The market seemed pretty weak in that line to me. I paid lovely and started for the door.

"Hurry back, now . . . you hear?"

I glanced back over my shoulder.

"Yeah, I hear."

I was still wondering what she meant when I got into the elevator after buying a paper at the lobby stand.

The bellboy with the sixth sense and who had anything was operating the lift. He stopped at the third floor.

"I'm five," I reminded.

"Please, Boss, folluh me, suh!"

There was nothing but urgency in those big eyes. I followed him. Down three doors, where he produced a passkey and jumped inside a room.

I walked in behind him.

"Boss, ah don' know if you is in trouble or if you ain't, but ah ain't fo'gittin' that twen'y."

"I wouldn't, if I were you." I didn't like this. "What's so secret?"

"Mistuh, *ah* don' know what's happenin'. Ah does know theahs two deetecktives in yo' room—not countin' ouah house dick."

"Oh-oh. I see."

"Boss, ah don' want you mad wif me but mebbe it's mah fault. See, suh, ah wus tellin' Jack—Jack he woiks the secon' flo'—'bout dat twenty an' how you done give it t' me an' this heah house dick he ovahheahed us talkin' an' gits s'picious on accounta he seen how you look when you fust come in, an' he 'cides he gon' take hissef a look in yo' room, an' up he go. Fust thing ah known heah comes two mo' deetecktives—f'm th' city—an' they is all in yo' room r'at now, an' if that desk clu'k saw me bringin' you up they is gon' be heah in 'bout a minnit, and you bettah go if they is som'p'm wrong an' if they ain't, *excuse me, suh!*"

His eyes were rolling in perfect harmony with the pain in my head.

"Quick! Where's the fire escape?"

I heard feet pounding down stairs and somebody began to rap on a door down the hall. Too close for meditation.

"Out th'oo dat bathroom window, Boss! Oh, Lawdy, ah sho' wuz a-prayin' you had jus' bin lucky in a hones' pokah game, suh."

He was scared. Hell, who wasn't? I wanted to get back to my room and pick up the loot but I knew better. That was out, over and done. I heard a shout in the hall but couldn't make out the words. Half of me was squeezing through the small window and reaching for the fire escape.

I made it; started down in a mad dash. A shot exploded above and behind, and rust showered from the second floor landing. I picked up speed to see if I could outrun the next one. I hit the ground and I hit it running. Another shot. Another near miss. They needed more time on the firing range.

I threw a quick look back and saw a heavy figure carefully backing down the fire escape. I hadn't realized the steepness of those steps myself. The next shot was the closest of the lot and urged me to move faster yet toward the end of that alley. As I neared the street junction I was mad with the hope they hadn't had the sense to have it covered.

They hadn't.

A taxi came rolling along the street just as if I'd made previous arrangements. I abandoned a lifelong inhibition right there—I loved women drivers now, because this cabbie was a female.

"Where to, Sir?"

"The railroad station," I said, "I have to catch a train."

CHAPTER FOUR

Donald Knowles

We was goin' back to Dallas to let El off at the bus station.

Junior, he was settin' there drivin' just cool as you please, an' me, I didn't have a worry in the world. Money in the towsack itchin' to get spent an' I was itchin' to spend it.

Junior put the brakes on 'bout a block from the bus station.

"Git out, El," he said. "You better walk the rest o' the way."

"But that's dang nigh a block off, Junior."

"That don't make me no never mind. Ain't takin' no chances. Git!"

El clumb out an' started a-hoofin' it down the sidewalk toward the station. Junior was smart. I reckon there ain't nobody's got a big brother much smarter'n mine. We headed on down the street an' I could tell somethin' was on Junior's mind.

"Donald. Me an' you, we got to split up a while."

"You done told me that, Junior. But not yet, huh? Cain't you wait a spell an' help me pick out some new clo'es afore you leave?"

"We'll see 'bout it."

He didn't say no more an' purty soon he turned in at a parkin' lot an' I knew he wasn't goin' to say no more about us busting up for a while. This was a nice big lot. The little old office wasn't no bigger'n a outhouse, but it was sure fixed up a lot purtier. When Junior stopped a man in white overalls come out of the little buildin'.

24

"How long you gonna be?" he ast Junior.

"Figger that's owin' to how long I wanta be," Junior snapped right back. He don't take nothin' offa nobody. He's allus been touchy like that. The man opened the door on Junior's side.

"I'll park it," he said.

"I'll park it," Junior said, an' he did.

He pulled over in a empty space which put some more cars 'twixt the LaSalle and the street. He cut the engine off an' just set there. He didn't say nothin' to me 'bout gettin' out, so I set there too. I'd just do whatever Junior said do.

"Donald, here's what. You go down the street an' git two suitcases—buy 'em. When you got 'em come straight back. We'll put our money in 'em. We ain't about to mosey down no city street totin' a towsack fulla greenbacks. I'll stay right in the car with the money 'til you git back."

He handed me a roll of them bran' spankin' new bills an' I stuffed it in the pocket of my jeans. I started to get out.

"Donald. Tell me back what I toldja to do," Junior said.

I did. I ain't near's dumb as he thinks I am, but I learn't long ago it's best to go 'long with Junior. He just likes to make sure 'bout things an' I reckon he's right.

'Cordin' to the signs at the corners, I went down Commerce Street. There was lotsa nice stores along an' I guess I wanted ever'thing I seen, but I didn't piddle none, 'cause I knew Junior wouldn't like settin' there waitin' in the parkin' lot. I come to a store that didn't have nothin' but leather stuff in the windows, an' went in. A man that was mostly face an' was rubbin' his hands like they was damp come up to me.

"Looking around, my boy?"

"I'm a-lookin' some."

"Maybe I can help you?"

"I wanta buy me some grips to put clo'es in."

He was a lanky guy an' he turned around an' stretched up on a high shelf an' drug down some grips that was mostly cardboard. A dumbbell coulda toll they wasn't real leather just by lookin'. I didn't even ast how much they was.

"I don't want them kind," I said. "I gotta have purty real-leather bags."

His face grinned at me by one corner of the mouth reachin' hard for his ear an' the other side stayin' put. He was a-gettin' me mad and I didn't know what in thunder ailed him that he was so thickheaded.

"I said I want somethin' good. Ain'tcha got no nice bags?"

That fetched him around. He went to the other side of the store an' I follered right along. He showed me a real good bag, all saddle leather with purty toolin' on it an' zippers on both sides.

"How do you like this one?"

I slid one zipper down to open one side an' there is three bottles an' little cups, an' a corkscrew even. Just the thing for a man travelin' in Oklahoma. I closed it an' slid the other one back—an' inside was one o' them fancy sets with places for ever'thing an' a space for clo'es.

"This is what I'm a-huntin'. One more just like this'n."

"Those are one hundred dollars each." He give me that lopsided smilin' look ag'in. "Do you wish to write a check. . . ?"

"I don't know nothin' about checks," I told him. "I allus pay cash."

I dug out the roll of money an' wondered what made him look so silly. Looked like his eyes was gonna pull right outta his head.

"Never you mind wrappin' 'em up—I'll carry 'em as is."

I counted out two hunderd dollars while he was writin' out a ticket showin' he sold 'em. He give me the ticket an' taken the money. I took on out, leavin' him a-countin' it for the second time. The fool was still shakin' his head the last time I seen him—I reckon maybe he was wishin' he'd a-charged me more. Sure was a funny guy to be workin' in such a swell store.

I went back to where Junior was waitin' on me. He took one look at them bags an' he smiled all over.

I stood watchin' while he packed the money in. He didn't ast me to help. Then I showed Junior the paper with the price on it an' the place where the whiskey bottles was under the other zipper. He laughed.

"Boy," he said, "we're eatin' high off'n the hog."

Right off he wanted to get some likker an' put in the bottles. So did I, so we picked our bags up an' walked offa the lot an' on down the street lookin' for a likker store. There's lotsa likker stores in Dallas. We went in one an' Junior bought three bottles of the highes' price drinkin' whiskey the guy had. We started to fill the little bottles, but the man chased us out. Seems like they got some kinda law ag'in openin' a bottle in the same place you buy it.

But we found a alley an' went in a little ways an' Junior opened up one of the bottles an' was pourin' easy so as not to spill ary drop—an' a cop comes up!

When I seen him I wasn't happy no more. Ever'thing come back to me like a mule kickin' you in the stomach, an' I wondered what in the world that cop'd do if he seen all that money.

"What're you doin', boys?" I was glad he didn't sound put out with Junior an' me, yet.

"Iff'n you look right close't you'll see I'm pourin' whiskey outta this bottle inta *this* bottle," Junior said.

"I can see that all right. Nice luggage you got there. Have much trouble boardin' freights with it?"

Junior quit pourin' an' looked the cop over, holdin' the bottle right side up by the neck. He was mad. I was scared he'd start something.

"We doin' somethin' ag'in the law?"

"Well, not exactly, I guess. Just one question though—where'd you buy those bags?"

"Donald. Show him the bill the guy give you at the store."

I dug the paper outta my jeans and handed it to the cop. He read it slow an' give it back to me like it was hard to believe. Then he walked away, still shakin' his head. I don't know if it was somethin' about us or somethin' wrong with them people in Dallas, but all of 'em shook their heads ever time they left us or we walked away.

Junior went on fillin' them bottles like nothin' happened. He didn't waste ary drop he was so steady, an' when he was through he zipped up the bags.

"Hongry, Donald?"

"Sure am—allus as when I ain't et breakfast an' missed supper the night before too, like now."

"Le's put on the feedbag, then."

We walked on down the street lookin' for a restrunt. We started by a pawnshop but didn't make it on accounta Junior seein' the pistols in the window. He sure likes guns. He looked for a spell an' then started in.

"Reckon I better git me a pistol," he said.

He bought a nice one an' didn't have no trouble with the man, but when he wanted the big black-leather blackjack the man give him some lip.

"What you gonna use it for?" he ast.

"Reckon 'at's my bizness," Junior said.

"Then it's my business not to sell it."

Junior studied a minute an' I know he wanted that there blackjack mighty bad.

28

"I'm jus' gonna kill hawgs with it down at the farm."

It hurt Junior to lie to the feller.

The man handed over the blackjack an' said, "Well, why didn't you say so?"

Junior paid him for the pistol an' blackjack an' a box of shells, an' we went on out ag'in to look for someplace to eat. I wanted a pistol too, but with Junior awready mad over the lip he took I thought I just better keep shut for a spell.

We found us a restrunt an' ordered double sizes of ham an' eggs, an' cold beer to wash 'em down. We set our bags under the table. My feet was on both sides of mine, just feelin' it an' likin' it.

"Donald, soon's we've et we'll git us some clo'es. Long's we got these work clo'es on we're gonna be ast questions by ever fool Texan sees us—"

I washed a big mouthful of right good salty ham down my gullet with half a glass of beer an' didn't say nothin'.

We went to this men's store after we'd et. We bought suits an' the all the trimmins'—from the skin out'ards. I got me a yeller shirt an' Junior made me git a suit that was dark brown. It fit with the shirt, awright, but I wanted me one with more color in it. I didn't nag Junior for it though, 'cause I was thinkin' to myself I still had a *little* money yet an' I could buy any dang thing I was a-wantin' to later.

Junior, he bought hisself a white shirt with a blue suit, and one of them new-fangled hand-painted ties. That there tie cost five dollars but it looked real good on him. That blue suit an' all-colored tie set off Junior's yeller hair just so. We stood lookin' in a lookin-glass at ourselfs in them new clo'es an' you could tell we was brothers even if he was a head taller'n me.

We was like two other people when we left that store. We went back to the restrunt where we et an' Junior ordered two beers an' when we got 'em he told me to listen. Like I was ever doin' much of anything else if he was talkin'.

"Donald. El's went. I been makin' a few changes in my plans. It's like this here: Me an' you, we're gonna stay right here in Dallas, I'm gonna send for Leonie to come on down here. We'll git us a apartment or a house an' git jobs payin' good an' stay right in this ol' town. I ain't gonna work no farm no more an' you ain't neither. Me an' Leonie can git hitched."

"We got to git jobs—with all this money?"

"Banks keeps money. We'll let 'em keep our'n. Mine, leastaways. You can do whatever with your'n, but iff'n you live with me an' Leonie you gotta pay rent—jes' like any boarder hasta. Iff'n you're smart, which you ain't, you'll put yore money in the bank, too. I don't mean all in one place. Put some here an' some yonder. Spread it out, like. Ain't nothin' in Dallas but banks, an' insurance sellers, nohow."

"I don't care, Junior. Whatever you say—only I wanta have some fun, too, outta this money, an' I cain't see no good of it layin' in banks."

"You gotta learn to keep money an' have fun too, Donald. You're gittin' to be a man, now."

"Awright, Junior. Whatever you think."

"You got a good hold on yoreself now, Donald—what with yore new clo'es an' yore belly full?"

"Sure, Junior. I'm feelin' good, now."

"Good thing. I killed that li'l towheaded gal at the tourist camp."

I couldn't harly believe what he said. My stummick drawed up even if it was full an' I felt like I was gonna be sick. Tears come to my eyes an' I couldn't talk. I know he done it like he said but I didn't wanta believe it. But he don't never lie an' don't know how.

"Stop yore blubberin', Donald. It's gone an' did an' I had to. It was her or me an' you an' El. I wouldn't a-toldja but I had to 'cause you was gonna find out anyway. Now quit."

I tried to stop cryin, an' I did after a minute or two. I just set there lookin' at him.

"Donald. You awright now?"

I just nodded my head up an' down. I still couldn't talk.

"I'm goin' back out to that there tourist camp. I don't like to mess around out there—it ain't healthy. But I gotta git that gal an' take her somewheres an' bury her, deep. In some place where nobody'd never find her. Understand?"

I understood, awright, but I could just see that little girl. I could see her a-hangin' onta my hand. I sure wished he hadn't done what he done. I wondered how he done it but I couldn't ast him. But I had to say what he wanted me to.

"I understand, Junior."

"Well, the sooner the better so I better be a-goin'. You wait on me right here, Donald. An' take it slow on the beer guzzlin'—we cain't git drunk yet. You hear me?"

"I'll stay here, Junior."

"I mean about beer guzzlin'."

"I won't."

"Okay. I won't be gone too long. Keep yore trap plumb shet 'cept to ast for whatcha want, you hear?"

"Sure, I ain't gonna say nothin' to nobody."

I looked up in a minute an' Junior was gone. I ordered another beer an' drunk it, slow, 'cause it didn't taste good no more. Just somethin' cold goin' down my throat.

Somebody bumped my arm, goin' by me to set down in the empty seat Junior had left. I started to tell 'em to watch out where they was goin', but I seen it was a girl. Besides, she was a-smilin' at me real nice an' was a purty little heifer. Too much powder an' colorin' smeared over her face, but purty.

31

I was afraid she wasn't gonna speak, but she did.

"Whatcha cryin' about?" she ast.

"I ain't cryin'."

"I'm sorry—I thought so. "

"Well, I ain't."

She reached over an' ran the ends of her fingers acrost the back of my hand.

"All right, honey. You ain't. I could stand a beer."

I knocked my glass on th' table an' stuck up two fingers for beer. When the guy brought it over an' the girl lifted her glass to drink it she looked at me acrost the top like maybe I was really somethin'.

She downed the beer like she was real thirsty.

"Lonesome, honey?" she ast me.

"Naw, I ain't lonesome."

"I am—real lonesome."

"Well, now, I'm right sorry, ma'am. You can set here an' talk to me. I'm a-waitin' for my brother."

"This's not very comfortable, is it?"

"Good enough for me."

"Why don't we go up to my room?" she said, and she was twiddlin' with my hand ag'in. Texas people don't never seem to hear what I say.

"I said I was a-waitin' for my brother."

"You can wait up there. He can come up afterwards. The bartender knows where it is."

Them fingers was up under my chin now, an' I guess I was a-wishin' they had more room to wander around in, sorta.

"I better not," I told her, but 'fore I thought some more words slipped outta my mouth. "Where you live?"

"In a nice room. Handy. Right next door in the Crescent Hotel, honey."

"Well, I might like to see your room. An' since you're so lonesome maybe I could just go up a little while and cheer you up, maybe."

"Oh, you are sweet, honey. I knew you would be when I saw you sittin' here lookin' so sad."

She was up an' rarin' to go. I stood up, knowin' Junior wasn't due back for a spell an' I couldn't see no harm. Junior'd prob'ly call me dumb if I was to walk off an' leave a girl I had eatin' right out of my hand. An' this little girl was plenty nice lookin' even if she did have too much junk on her face an' was a little bit older'n me.

I took aholt of my bag of money an' started for the door. She got the bartender to look at her.

"When his brother comes back, tell him he's with me." The bartender helt up his right hand, makin' a circle with his thumb an' finger.

She helt open the door for me, an' I walked on out.

33

CHAPTER FIVE

Bill Brown

I rode the front four inches of the rear seat, twisting around and looking through the window–ready to hit the floorboards at the first flash of exploding powder in some eager cop's gun.

I sat that way for a block and a half, and took a big breath of relief when nothing happened. The fact that there wasn't even a car trailing the taxi convinced me I had, for a while, eluded the pride of Dallas.

"Why'ntcha, relax, Mister? I don't ever have accidents any more."

"Huh? Oh . . . just not used to lady taxi drivers, I guess."

"Don't girls drive the cabs where you come from?"

"Not many. By the way, I've changed my mind. Drop me at the bus station, will you?"

"Which bus station?"

"The Greyhound. . . . This isn't a very friendly town, is it?"

"Oh, I wouldn't say that, Mister. Depends on what kind of friends you like, I guess."

"No, I guess you wouldn't look at it exactly like I do."

"Where you from?"

"Montana."

She rolled to a smooth stop at the bus station. I read the meter and paid her.

I circled around the bus station looking for the cause of my recent rise in blood pressure. I spotted him through the window and even on casual observation he was a very, very sad hick. He was standing near the lockers and as I watched he walked over and looked in an empty one with the look on a kid's face when you make a coin disappear right in front of his eyes. He was tugging at the red lobe of his ear and wiping sweat off his forehead between jerks. A coin had disappeared for him, all right. A lot of coin.

I eased into the station and walked up and tapped him on the shoulder from his blind side.

"Pardon me, fellow, but didn't you get the wrong key?" I asked him, and smiled pleasantly into the yellow eyes.

He jumped and sputtered, and I guess the shave fooled him for a second–then the eyes lit up like two neon tubes.

"I shore did, Mister, and I'm shore glad to see you, let me tellya."

I could believe the guy. Relief in the folds of his face would have done credit to a Democrat just informed of his election in spite of a thumbs-down from Franklin D.

"Suppose we go outside where we can talk, friend."

"Nothin' for us to talk about. Shucks, I ain't mad about that little mistake. I made mistakes in my time, too, I reckon. So jus' you hand me the right key an'. . . ."

"Let's go outside."

I'd taken the smile off and the way I said it made a believer of him. The loose, blubbery lips pursed out and a thinking slit was laboriously drawn between his eyes.

"Guess it ain't no harm in talkin'."

He followed me out and I walked a few doors down and found a storefront with a "FOR RENT" sign hung in the window. He guided easily and we stepped into the alcove.

I had him steered into just about the right position and I started a low one–not hard but a little nasty–and sunk my fist two or three inches into his underbelly below the beltline.

He took it fairly good for a man his age and didn't even fold up, but his breathing ran into bad trouble. It came hard, in shuddering gasps that lasted a minute and then slowed down till it was almost regular.

"Where'd you get the money?"

I pulled my fist back to bury it in the same spot. But he held his hand up to signal he'd tell me when he got his breath. I waited one more minute and he was breathing easy enough to get words out.

"What money?" he croaked.

I shoved the first two fingers of my right hand into his big nose and pushed viciously upward. Yellow eyes were swimming in tears as he backed up under the pressure of the stiff fingers reaching through his head for his brain.

He backed into the plateglass window and was stopped short.

"Where'd you get the money?"

I jerked the fingers out of his nose and the way he groaned and grabbed for it they must have hurt as bad coming out as going in. I wiped my fingers on the lapels of his coat. His nose was bleeding nicely.

"It's ransom money," he said.

He spit it out along with a little blood and seemed to be pretty bitter about the position he was in.

"Don't put yore fingers in my nose no more, Mister—that hurts!"

"Interesting. I know a few tricks that hurt worse, too. If you don't explain in full about the money I'll begin showing you a few."

I pretended to reach for him again and he was panic stricken. He blurted out the wildest tale I ever heard—and I've listened to a lot of mad fairy stories in the department in L.A. But this yarn was just fantastic enough to have a ring of truth. I couldn't ignore the fact I'd seen close to five thousand dollars in cash. Considering this clown's general appearance, it had without doubt come to him from some crooked source.

"Where's that little girl you're talking about now?"

"Junior done tied her up and left her out where we stayed. She ain't hurt, ary bit. Shucks, 'at kid liked it with us—Donald buyin' her ice cream and her a-callin' him uncle an' ever'thing."

"Don't tell me how sweet it all was. Just tell me the location of the motel you stayed in."

He told me—with such detailed directions he had to be telling the truth. For a guy in as deep as he was, he was certainly free with his information. I was unhappy to hear all of this detail but I realized it was necessary. Otherwise I couldn't have known what a real jam I'd got into and I might have done something quite foolish. The more he talked the deeper in I got.

He couldn't know it, of course, but everything pointed to me. Bill Brown, a fresh name on a hotel register, with a pile of ransom money in my room—probably marked bills, at that. I could see rough times ahead for that same Bill Brown.

I could clear myself in time, I was sure, but time was the commodity I couldn't afford. By the time they released me I'd be tied in with the news I was expecting from L.A. Then I'd be a free boarder of the City of Dallas until extradition papers could be cleared to take me back to L.A.—for trial, that is. A cute set-up!

The pain in my head didn't blind me to the only way out. The hard way, but the only way. I couldn't run and dodge with that hotel register following me around the world in my own handwriting. My only bet was to gather this band of comic-book kid snatchers, all three of them. I'd turn them in with the confession which I felt very capable of obtaining at the moment, and then I'd get the hell out of Dallas. I could start by making a deal with this talkative one.

"Listen, Pop. I'm not a policeman. I'm just a nice guy looking for a simple way to make some money. It happens that just now I have some of your money. You'd like to have it back—in fact you'd be very happy if you could get half of it back. . . Am I right, so far?"

"Me, I'd be some happier if you'd plain turn me a-loose."

"Okay, Pop—go ahead. I won't stop you. Just forget the money."

He stayed where he was and didn't move anything but his thick lips.

"How'm I gonna know you'd gimmie half o' my money back?"

"Our money, you mean? You'll get it. All you have to do is to help me get my hands on the other ten grand. Then—and only then—you'll got your half. Is that fair?"

"Naw . . . it ain't what I'd call fair. But I don't wanta git back to Oklahoma with jus' two hunderd dollars, after havin' all that there money once't."

He shouldn't have said that, but some people never learn. I took the roll of bills away from him.

"Okay, Pop. We've got to keep all our eggs in my basket so I can trust you. You help me get the ten grand and half of this roll comes to you along with our other deal."

"I done toldja I'd help! Ain't no call to take *all* my money."

"So you'll help me, and here's what you're going to do: Somehow, and I don't care how, you get these partners of yours back to the bus station. I'll ask them for the rest of the ransom money when I talk with them. I'll be persuasive. That's when you get your part, when I get their part. Can you manage to do that?"

"Shore, I can do it, awright. But I'm a-tellin' you one thing, Mister. You better git a mighty good story to tell Junior. He likes his money an' ain't likely to lissen to nobody who's tryin' to take it off'n him."

"You fix it so I can talk to them. I'll worry about the rest."

"You're a-bitin' off a big chaw of worryin'."

"Get started. I'll meet you at the bus station, one hour from now."

He walked around me, keeping his distance as if he thought I might plant another one on him for emphasis, and shuffled off up the sidewalk.

I felt like he would round up this rough-and-ready Junior he described and the younger deadhead. Those two should be very happy to see me when they heard I knew all about their little party and the new business they were in. Happy enough to crush my skull if they got a chance. But I'd worry about that when. The hick hadn't helped my headache a bit in exposing my situation to me, and it was hard to think straight. Maybe I could grind out some idea later about stepping out of the mess. Right now I had to get out to that motel and untie the little girl and see that she got home safe and sound—if she was really alive.

The hick had seemed pretty sure of Junior's mean disposition, and if he was still hanging around in Dallas after all he'd pulled I was a little doubtful he'd left the little girl in any condition to talk. And why had they stayed in Dallas after the pay-off? How could anyone think with the off-key hammering of a Chinese gong that was going on in my head?

I whistled at the first taxi that passed. Another woman driver, but I got in anyhow. Might as well live dangerously.

"Start for Fort Worth."

She did, with a nice big lurch, which seemed to loosen a running, dull, and unprompted chatter about the traffic situation in Dallas. She bluffed everything from semis down to English Austins out of her way. I guess she was bluffing—at least she didn't get called and have to show her hand.

The motel the old man had described was easy to spot. A row of decrepit shacks which had that occupied-one-hour-five-times-a-night look. I let her go about two hundred yards past it before I tapped her on the shoulder.

"Let me out here."

She squealed rubber all over the highway and I nearly joined her in the front seat. Even if I didn't have business in the neighborhood I would still have been relieved to part company with that female Barney Oldfield.

"I thought you were goin' to Fort Worth."

"I was. But the thought of leaving Dallas is just more than I can bear."

I paid her and waited at a safe distance while she slid the cab around on the gravel shoulder and gunned it in the direction of Dallas. Then I took off my coat and started walking across a ploughed field between me and the motel. I circled in behind the row of shacks and was able to pick out Number Sixteen.

If that farmer had been lying, I knew I was in for more trouble.

I walked quietly along the row, stopped back of Sixteen and listened. Nothing. I tried the rear door. It was locked. So was the screen on the window, but it was old and rusty. It only took a second to pry it out some with my fingers, enough to get a grip. I had already made too much noise to start being careful so I tore it off with a rending jerk. The window slid up easily. I moved it to the top, and using both hands on the sill I threw myself up and inward, headfirst. But I don't know if I ever got inside or not.

Flames and bells and Roman candle shells exploded, in a wondrous mixture which seemed to center for an instant in the ever-present ache in my head, and for a fleeting moment a fiery leer swam through the red haze. Something had happened to my head, and it wasn't there any more.

CHAPTER SIX

JUNIOR KNOWLES

I walked purty fast an' it never taken me long to git back to the parkin' lot.

I paid the smart-aleck in the white overalls for lettin' us park. Reckon he makes lots o' money, chargin' a man to let a car set a little while like he done. I figgered that might be a good bizness for me an' Donald to git into, with me handlin' the money an' Donald parkin' the cars. Had to git us some way to make money. But right now I had to cover up the way I'd got the money we done had.

"I guess you'll drive it out yourself?" the feller said.

"Yore guessin's better'n what it was when I come in."

I pulled her out an' kicked up as much fuss as I could goin' by the li'l office. I never liked that there feller for some reason. He give me a dirty look an' I jes' laughed in his face and drove on inta the street.

I went back out the way we come to town an' started out the road tords the place where the gal was stuck away in the closet. When I come to the tourist camp I pulled in an' stopped, with the engine still a-runnin. We hadn't been gone long, considerin', so I never figgered the manager woulda

cleaned the cabin up yet. But one thing was a-worryin' me
some—I wish't I hadn't of throw'd that key up on his porch,
'cause now I was gonna hafta ast him for it back. No way to
git around it. I knocked on his door an' kept one hand close
to the blackjack in my hip pocket in case anything could be
wrong.

He was so long gittin' to the door I begin to git nervous, but
I reckon he was jes' slow, 'cause he finally showed up.

"Where's my key?" I ast him.

Reckon my new clo'es throwed him.

"I don't know you," he said.

"I stayed in Number Sixteen last night, an' I forgot somethin'. I wanta git it."

"You the feller who left that key on the porch?"

"I never seen no use gittin' outta the car an' botherin' you
when we was all paid up. C'mon an' gimmie the key—won't
take me but two shakes to git what I want outta there."

"I think I rented that cabin already. Just a minute. . . ."

"Never mind, iff'n it's rented. I wouldn't wanta bother
nobody."

I was tryin' to figger out what I'd do if there was people in
that there cabin. It would shore make gittin' a body outta
there a hard nut to crack.

"No, it ain't," the man said. "They checked out. Got some
pretty regular couples from the honkytonks 'round here that
don't never stay very long."

"They give you anything they found in the cabin?"

"Nope, nothin'. If somethin's stole it ain't my fault, neither.
You can look for yourself. Here's the key—but bring it right
back, you hear?"

"Don't worry none. What would I do with yore key?"

I pulled the car down close to the front door of the cabin
an' went in. I felt a lot better now, 'cause if the people that

used the cabin had found that kid stuffed in the closet they'd
a-been hollerin' yet.

When I checked up to make shore, she was in there awright.
I drug her out an' was fixing to wrap her in a blanket, when a
rattlin' come from the back door that drawed my stummick
up into a ice cube.

I moved quick. I put the gal on the bed, easy an' quiet, an'
tiptoed tords the back. I stood right still in the li'l kitchen. I
heard the screen rip off the back window, an' knowed then
somebody was a-payin' me a call.

With my new blackjack in my hand I moved over an' stood
by that window. The blackjack was solid an' hard an' heavy
in my hand. The window slid up an' a great big black-headed
feller dove in head first, gittin' up to 'bout his beltline on the
window.

I doughpopped him right on the back of the head behind
his ear. S'prised me when it never knocked him right out, but
he shaken his head a time or two an' hung on. Then I hit him
ag'in an' that done for him. He was colder'n a Panhandle
blizzard. Seein' as how he wanted in so bad, I drug this feller
over the windowsill an' I dumped him in a big heap on the
floor.

Runnin' my hands over him I found out he never had no
gun nor nothin'. Wouldn't be no cop, comin' in the back
window an' 'ithout no kinda gun. But who in tarnation was
he an' what was he after? I reckoned he musta been breakin'
in to see what he could steal. Well, he shore picked a pore
time–'cause I was thinkin' of a different use for him.

He was jes' what I was a-needin'. What the movin' pitchers
calls a fall guy. Idys hit me so fast at times I don'no how I
keep up with 'em. Here he was, cold turkey in my hands
'thout no invitation. When he woke up he'd have a kidnappin'

an' killin' hung around him so tight a wiggle'd cut him in two.

To make shore he'd stay put a while I clipped him ag'in behind his ear.

Then I walked out an' went back to the office to see the manager. Couldn't chance nobody comin' inta that cabin 'fore I was done. I banged on the door an' he showed up after a bit. He poked his head out an' I told him what I was a-wantin'.

"Reckon I'll stay another night," I said, and shoved some rent at him.

"Find what you was huntin'?" he ast.

"Yeah, it was right in the closet where I'd left it."

"It'll be one-fifty apiece more—that is, if yore friends are stayin' on with ya."

"You don't see no friends, do you? Jes' me. They got sense an' went home, after spendin' one night in a dump like this here."

"Nobody forcin' ya to stay here, Mister. If ya don't like the place. . . ."

"Shet up an' gimmie the change. I shore ain't come here to gab with you."

He seen I meant bizness an' give me the change. Back at the cabin I tapped this overgrowed Tyrone Power ag'in. I liked hittin' him, but I never wanted to kill him or he'd miss out on his fun with them Dallas cops.

When I picked the kid up to dump her in the blanket I seen she was gittin' a little stiff, 'cept for her neck which let her head roll around like the crank on a T-Model Ford. But she wasn't much to handle an' when I had her all wrapped up I threwed her in the back seat of the car. It wasn't so easy with the big feller with blood clotted on the back of his head.

He was heavier an' harder to handle than a loose bale of alfalfa. I got him in, though, 'thout nobody seein' nothin'. I locked the cabin door an' drove the LaSalle out inta the highway.

Findin' the house where the kid had useta live taken me longer'n I'd figgered on an' I begin to worry 'bout Donald setting in that cafe waitin' on me. I wasn't sure I shoulda left him by hisself.

I finally found the place—out a piece from Dallas in some park section. It was a big house settin' 'way back from the street with a big front yard. It had one o' them curvin' driveways where you pull up in front by a big porch with great big posts holdin' up another li'l porch up above. It sure was a rich-folks' house, awright, an' I was sorry I hadn't ast for more'n I did.

I never used that driveway, though. Too close for comfort. I jes' pulled over an' parked ag'in the curb at the street. My window-buster from the tourist camp was snorin' away on the floorboards in the back. I'd a-liked to put him under the steerin' wheel but was afeared to make any fuss. He'd never be able to explain anyways 'cause he never knew what happened hisself. Iff'n a guy cain't prove to the cops what he's been doin', he's jes' natcherly been doin' the things they cain't explain to the newspapers. Any fool knows cops do that.

When I couldn't see nobody nor no car nowhere I jes' walked away, not wishin' that feller no luck in gittin' outta the mess I'd stuck his neck into. He was prob'ly bein' hunted for a hunderd other things by the cops anyhow.

Me an' Donald we could go on 'bout our bizness now, an' the cops would prob'ly hang that big man.

Couple of blocks down the street I got to thinkin' about him tryin' to answer questions durin' one o' them there third degrees—with rubber hosin' an' all them bright lights a-shinin' in his eyes an' him a-wantin' a cigarette or a drink o' water

45

they wouldn't give him an' it was so funny to me I got to laughin' an' laughin', like a dang fool. Reckon he'd think twice't 'fore he tried breakin' in a tourist cabin ag'in.

I found a sign which said it was a bus stop an' got on the first bus that come along. That was smart, 'cause it wasn't more'n three-four mile downtown, an' iff'n I'd a got a taxi the driver'd be more apt to remember one passenger than a bus driver would. All I had to do now was go git Donald an' we'd be in the tall cotton.

Wasn't but a few minutes till I was in the cafe where Donald was s'posed to be waitin' for me. But the dam fool wasn't even there, an' neither was his bag. I was throwed for a minute, an' I seen red. Mister Donald Knowles was gonna hafta learn I was boss an' that what I said went. I bought a beer an' cooled off some while I was a-drinkin' it, cause I knowed Donald wanted to stay as close to me as he could. I never thought he'd be mad enough about the killin' of the li'l gal to start out by hisself. He prob'ly wasn't far away. I'd jes' wait an' maybe he'd be back after a bit.

The bartender kept lookin' at me, an' then at my bag with the money in it. I never liked that none too good.

"Whatsa matter with you," I ast, "ain't you never seen a suitcase before?"

"Oh, it ain't that. But a young guy in here a while ago left a message with me for his brother. You kinda look like him, and he had a bag sorta like that one."

"What'd he look like?"

"Well, sort of frail lookin', not tall as you, but his hair was pretty much the same color."

"What kinda clo'es?"

"I didn't notice—a suit, but I don't remember what color it was."

"That's my brother. What'd he tell you to tell me?"

"Well, he left here with Madge. She's a . . . girl that works outta here. Got a room in the hotel next door—that way. Said you could come up there or wait here, whichever you want."

"Much obliged."

Just like my fool brother, I thought. But I hadta laugh. Nigger rich, an' he jes' couldn't wait to spend some o' his money on the first splittail what come along.

"My brother drink much 'fore he left?" I ast.

"Naw, not much. They had a beer together and I sold him one 'fore she come in. He wasn't nothin' like drunk, but he was a little dazed about Madge, looked like."

"He would be, yeah."

"Well, it's no disgrace—that gal's a pretty smooth dish and a good operator."

When he said "operator" it made me uneasy. S'posin' she operated a bunch of talk outta Donald, or seen the money in his bag? That could cause a lotta trouble. I never figgered Donald would talk too much iff'n he wasn't drunk. Then it hit me.

Donald had plenty of likker with him to stay drunk for a couple of days!

An' feelin' bad like he was when I left an' not too much sense a-workin on his side neither, he might do jes' that. Iff'n he did git drunk an' start talkin' in front o' that gal.

"What's that there gal's room number, bartender?"

"Three-oh-three. If you go up, tell her I sentcha."

"Tell her yoreself."

I was hopin' Donald never told her nothin'. An' I hoped she hadn't acted smart an' found out nothin' for herself. I reely hoped 'cause either way she learnt anything it was jes' too wet to plow.

It looks like a man, once't he's got hisself inta somethin big, keeps on gittin' in worser an' worser. People keep buttin' in

47

an' won't leave him alone, when all he needs is bein' left to hisself to git along. Looks as if he has jes' got to git in deeper an' deeper, first thing he knows he's got so deep he's in his grave an' a- reachin' up to pull the dirt in on top o' hisself.

Walkin' outta that café I shore wished Donald had done what I told him an' waited on me.

CHAPTER SEVEN

MADGE BAEDER

We were up in my hotel room before he knew he'd left the joint downstairs, I think.

He was a bashful kid, but that didn't keep him from having some pretty definite ideas. The first one was real cute, too. While I was watching to see what he'd do he took his coat off, folded it neatly, and laid it on the chair.

"You only got one chair?" he asked me, with a sly look.

"How many do you want?"

"Had to put my coat on the chair, so I reckon we'll just have to set on the bed."

He was as subtle as a Fort Worth cattleman. But now he started out to make me in a big way. He put his tie on the chair with his coat, and I noticed he loosened his shirt an extra button and pulled it apart so I could glimpse the few red hairs on his chest. He kicked off his shoes, sat on the edge of my bed and leaned back against the headboard.

"Still lonesome, gal?"

"Why, no, honey. I feel fine with you keeping me company."

"Well, c'mon over an' keep clos'ter company."

48

He threw his feet up toward the middle of the bed, scooted over to make room and patted the place where he wanted me to sit. I sat down by him and put my hand on his chest and leaned toward him.

"You don't talk much, huh?" he asked.

He was right, I realized. I was in a rut lately–if I didn't ply a guy with the usual professional questions, make a deal and get down to earning my fees as soon as he walked into my room, I wasn't much of a social success. Somehow right then I didn't feel too professional.

"Oh, sugar, I usually talk a lot. It's just that you being so nice has got me thinking a lot of things I shouldn't be thinking."

"I know a way to get us talkin'. You want a drink of likker?"

"I could stand one, honey–sure. But this place don't have service and I wouldn't want you to have to go after it."

"Never mind about the goin'. Slide that there bag of mine over here 'side the bed."

"Oh. Did you bring a bottle? I'll get it out for–"

"I'll git the likker, gal." His voice seemed sharp, but with him I couldn't tell. "You got a chaser?"

"A couple of cokes–but they're not cold."

He unzipped one side of his grip, watching me from under his eyelashes as he brought three fancy flasks and little matching silver cups into view. The little devil. He was just showing off.

"Git them cokes, gal, an' a coupla glasses. These here cups are purty but they don't hold nothin'."

I brought the glasses and opened the cokes. He mixed, with his idea of gestures, two highballs. That is, if you call a water glass two-thirds full of hundred-proof whiskey cut with an ounce of coke a highball.

"Well, I'll be! I ain't even ast what yore name is, gal. What do they call you 'round here?"

49

"My name is Madge, honey. . . . And I'd like to remember it, so how about a little more coke in this? You sure mix 'em strong."

"Shucks, Madge! We don't never worry 'bout mixin' likker up where I live. Most times we ain't got nothin' to chase it with. Just mixed this here cause I'm a-drinkin' with a lady."

"Where are you from?. . . And I guess you have a name, don't you?"

"I'm from Oklahoma. Name's Donald. Here's how, Madge."

He reached out to touch glasses with me, and it was important to him. We drank—me sipping, but the boy went all out. He lowered half that glass of whiskey before he stopped. But I felt the bed jerk as he had trouble holding back a cough. He was real game, though, and only that and the sudden moisture in his eyes gave him away. He was still showing off for me.

"Don't drink so fast, Donald. You make me feel like an awfully poor drinking partner."

"Uh. . . . Okay, Madge, I'll sorta wait on you if you want it that way. You know, you look purtier now than down there in the restrunt."

I sipped my drink, and it was better now that the extra coke had tamed it a little. I know what brought that speech of Donald's on—the light was softer in the room and kinder to my face.

"Maybe that's your whiskey talking," I said.

"Maybe. Maybe not."

His thoughts seemed to wander, and the sad look came back. I reached over and brushed his stiff hair with my hand until the shy smile came back into his eyes and lips. He really was a sweet looking boy that way, and I wanted to keep him cheerful. For just long enough I let my hand wander into the V of his shirt and excite the sparse growth that he was so proud of. Then I gave him a soft pat on the cheek to widen the grin a little more.

"Let me fix you another drink, honey. For a man like you one drink mustn't hold much kick."

He squirmed with pleasure at the attention he was getting, and I wondered again how so many wives have trouble keeping their men when it's so simple to please them. Sure, Donald was just a boy, but men stay boys all their lives when it comes to how they like to be treated. Who knows that better than me?

"Heck, Madge, you're shore a nice gal. Real settlin', bein' here with you."

I mixed us another drink, but not as strong as he'd made them. He toasted us again, and my drink had a hard time getting around the swelling in my throat. Funny how ever so often you've got to get a sample of things the way you'd like to have them—the things you kicked around until they are forever gone except for the heart-rending samples that keep rocking you back on your heels. Maybe I was a little drunk already. I certainly was soft today.

"I'm glad you like being with me, Donald."

"Ain't it a little stuffy in this here room, Madge?"

"Want me to fan you with a paper, Donald? The windows are wide open. Just no breeze today, honey."

"Naw, I don't want you a-fannin' me. I want you touchin' me. But we could get outta some o' those hot clothes, couldn't we?"

He'd finished his drink and I took his glass. Looking directly into his eyes, I started unbuttoning his shirt. One button at a time, letting my fingers touch the flesh beneath enough to be appreciated and not enough to be clumsy. It bothered him. What was a hell of a lot worse, it was bothering *me*.

He raised up and let me pull the shirt from under his belt and I took it off over his arms. Then I tossed it over on the chair and waited to see what he would do next.

"Ain't you hot in here, too, Madge?"

"Yes, Donald, a little bit."

Then I thought I'd help him some, he was trying so hard.

"My blouse, Donald . . . do you think it would be all right? It is stuffy in here."

"Why, shore, Madge—we're good enough friends a few old clo'es ain't nothin' to us. Turn around an' I'll unhook it for you, like you done for me."

I did as he said and his excited hands fumbled with the little buttons of my blouse. I cursed silently at the goose-pimples rising on the flesh of my arms.

He slipped the blouse down over my shoulders and as I let it slide off I sensed his fingers hovering, hesitating, over the fastener of my bra. But his nerve didn't hold out.

"Madge," he grunted, "fix us another drink, willya? A stiff one, this time."

"Sure, Donald. I'll rinse the glasses out first."

I mixed the drinks in the clean glasses and handed him one, which I intended to be his last. I didn't know how much beer he'd had in the cafe and I didn't want him going under. Not this boy.

He tossed the drink off too fast and handed me the glass back with a nod toward the flask we were working on. I tried to think how to delay giving him another one.

"Too much sun coming in, honey. I'll lower the shades a little."

I walked to the window and pulled the shade down about halfway and turned back intending to talk him out of drinking any more—hoping it would slip his mind while watching me.

He was watching me, all right—over the flask he had tilted up to his mouth taking the stuff straight. I got there too late.

It was empty when he let it fall to the rug as he tried to set it down. I'd miscalculated, and all of a sudden he was drunk. I was sore, and know it was because I'd wanted him to want me—sober. Now I'd waited too long and the whiskey got to him first.

He'd been so quiet and sweet, but now he started talking as fast as he could with his thick tongue. His babbling meant nothing to me at first, but when it began to sink in I got a shock. He was telling me some wild story about being a no-good kidnapper and a murderer and wishing he'd never left Oklahoma. He rambled and raved and I didn't know what in the world to make of it all. I tried to make him hush, but he was all mixed up and trying to straighten out something inside him, I could tell that.

Well, I'm certainly no angel inside either and the least I could do was try to keep this kid from going mad right in my room, anyway. I put my arms around him and started soothing him with talk the best I could.

That loosened the tears he was holding back and he laid his head on my breast and sobbed away like his heart was torn in two—great, shuddering sobs that shook him from head to toe. The patting and gentling that boy got from me would have made me the permanent laughing stock of Dallas. But cheering him up was the most important thing in the world right then. No matter what kind of trouble he was in.

After he cried it out I went to the bathroom and wet a rag and washed his face and eyes and cooled his forehead with it. He was watching my face with a haunted look in his eyes.

"You mus' figger I'm a awful dam' fool, Madge. Comin' up here an' shootin' off my mouth with a whole mess o' lies an' getting' you tore up about nothin'."

"Hush, Donald, honey. I don't think that; I just don't under-stand. What you said didn't make much sense, and everybody tells me their troubles."

He smiled at me sweet enough to break my own heart, and his eyes were heavy.

"You ain't gonna tell my brother the stuff I raved about, are you? He'd think I was goin' stark-starin' crazy."

"I don't know your brother, honey. And as far as I'm con-cerned you didn't tell me a thing."

I was wondering about that brother, though, and just how much of what Donald had said might have some truth in it. I was curious but not worried. I've been told enough things by men to have a dozen hanged and not less than a hundred ridden out of town on a rail if certain people know as much as I did about their recreational preferences.

"Come on, Donald, cheer up. You didn't murder anybody. Let's have fun together."

"Suits me, Madge. . . . Let's seal the bargain with a drink—straight outta one o' them other bottles."

I hesitated, but he seemed in better shape after his crying jag, and I didn't want to make him mad. So I took a small pull out of the flask and passed it to him. I had to reach and take it away from his lips, and he coughed up the heat. He was evidently trying to drown something. I took the rest of his clothes off and he giggled.

He looked so sweet lying there on his back with his eyes half-closed and grinning up at me I had to take time to cuddle him a little. God, he was cute. I leaned over to kiss him and he put his am around my neck and didn't want to let me go. It was a long kiss. Too damn long.

By the time it was finished the little stinker was sound asleep! Wouldn't you just know it? The only man I'd wanted in . . . oh, hell!

While I finished undressing I had to laugh. Stood up by the Sandman! Well, he'd wake up some time. Lying there beside him I went back over the stuff he'd been raving about.

Several pieces of the jigsaw started falling into place. Cute as Donald was, it was still plain that he was a hayseed who was not accustomed to fancy items like the grip he was carrying. Or those nice clothes, for that matter. He was too proud and anxious to show them off. And the fear of his big brother's temper hadn't been play-acting.

He'd been upset when I started to open the grip to get the whiskey. Why? Maybe he had his dirty clothes in it and was ashamed for me to see them. Then I sat bolt upright in bed.

Hadn't he said something about ransom money? Could that be in the bag? Pipe dreams. I lay back down and cuddled up to him. But Donald, passed out, limp and unresponsive, was not as interesting as Donald awake, shy, sweet and fumbling. I couldn't shut off my curiosity about that bag of his. If he would only wake up—but he wouldn't.

I had to face it. I wanted to know what was in the bag and only had one way of finding out. I rolled away from Donald and got up and walked around to his side of the bed, thinking if he woke up I could tell him I wanted a drink. I even went so far as to spill a stiff one into one of the glasses and poured the rest of one of the cokes in on top of it. Then I slid the zipper on the other side of the bag open.

Money. No clothes. Nothing *but* money—neatly stacked in fives, tens and twenties. I zipped the bag closed in a hurry and set it just like it was before I opened it. Then I grabbed for the drink and swallowed it like so much lemonade. I was weak in the knees, so I went back around the bed and crawled in beside Donald again. So it was true!

Blood money, or I wasn't Madge Baeder, Prostitute.

I tried not to let my thoughts get into the old rut, about how if I ever took enough dough off some sugar-daddy I would shake the dust of Dallas and this lousy racket off my heels.

I felt like I was still young, enough to go legit, but I'd need a long vacation to erase the hardness that had become part of me. Nobody had been willing to foot the bills for a thing like that. That bag standing beside the bed would foot a lot of bills if I could talk Donald into it. Maybe I could. Then I thought about his brother.

He'd stand by and watch his kid brother leave for parts unknown with me and a grip crammed full of ransom? He would not! I doubted if Donald would scram out of here with me without seeing his brother, either, because that brother seemed to be his own private idol.

Blood money . . . it had no identity and no legal title or ownership, except possession. Did anyone ever go to the cops and report the loss of money they'd collected in a kidnapping racket? Well, I'd been trying to dodge it, but there it was and I had to face it.

If I didn't? Donald would wake up after a while and we'd have a few minutes' temporary pleasure—it had been silly for me to think I could interest him permanently.

If I did? Would they find me and put a part in my throat? They would if I was handy. Their movements would be limited because they were being hunted themselves. I was beginning to jump at every sound in the hotel and realized I was expecting the big bad brother to pop in raising hell in general. I made up my mind in a hurry.

Once started I didn't waste any time, and Donald kept snoring away. Except for the bag I intended to borrow and a couple of changes, I was going to travel light, so it was a matter of minutes until I stood ready to leave, looking down at the sleeping boy. I had quite a battle with myself over leaving him that way.

I settled it by making a risky bet with myself. If he woke up I'd stay, if he didn't it just wasn't supposed to be for me and the kid.

I leaned over and pressed my lips against his—and I didn't short him on his odds.

It didn't even interrupt the discord he was sawing out. So I patted his cheek, picked up the bag that was my future and the other little one of my own and walked out, closing the door softly behind me. I wouldn't want him to wake up now that I'd gone this far.

I walked to the elevator and pushed the button. Me for the airport and the first plane west—a long way west. San Francisco, maybe . . . new clothes . . . a nice little apartment and a long rest . . . a new name and a fresh start.

CHAPTER EIGHT

Elsworth Mercer

... By God! That ain't no way to treat a dam' dog, let alone a human bein'. Stickin' fingers in a man's nose thataway is jus' about the meanes' thing a man can do to a man. Cinch I ain't never had nobody treat me meaner'n that blackheaded thief done. Stealin' all my money in my suitcase . . . an' then that wasn't enough! Oh, no! He even taken the little bit I had left. A-hittin' me in the stummick was bad . . . but worst of all was them big ol' stiff fingers gougin' in my nose plumb up to where it's too dang little for 'em to go. Nothin' but a danged Injun could be that mean. . . . Junior'll kill that big feller sure's God made little green apples. . . . An' I'm gonna stand an' look an' laugh when he does. I gotta find Junior. . . . Guess I been up an' down this here street fifty times or more. . . . I don'no where he's went. Mighta already took out from Dallas, an' iff'n he did it's jus' the end of ever'thing for me. It cain't be thataway—it jus' cain't! I cain't go back to Oklahoma 'thout no money. . . . I ain't even got my ol' car no more. Iff'n Junior was to give it back, which I reckon he never would, it'd only get me in more trouble. . . .

... Bet that dirty longfingered coward ain't aimin' to gimmie none o' my money back—not a dang penny, I bet. I wish I could shoot that feller, right where he hit me. . . . I'd stan' there cool as a cucumber in a bowl of icewater an' blow the smoke outta the gun while he died—an' laugh and laugh. . . . But iff'n I cain't find Junior an' Donald purty soon that big

58

devil's gonna be a-comin' back to the bus station–to see me. I don'no what I oughtta do. . . . Shoulda knowed better'n to give that big ape my suitcase in the first place. . . . Musta been plumb outta my fool head, the way I let him git it. An' I give him a nickel tip. By God, I did! I give him a tip–for stealin' my life's savin's right away from me!. . . An' him comin' 'round later to laugh at me an' stick his dam' dirty fingers up my nose. . . .

. . . I'm so dumb I need one o' them keepers like at the state 'sylum, stead o' bein' 'lowed to run around loose. They's something wrong in my head, I reckon. . . . Junior'll only tell me I'm a dang clabberhead iff'n I'm ever able to find him, an' it looks like I cain't. . . . Wonder if I could outsmart this feller I'm a-going' to meet an' git some o' my money off'n him? Maybe I could tell 'im Junior has went back to Oklahoma an' git him to go up there. Once't I had him in Oklahoma there might be some way. . . . Aw! I reckon sometimes a man'd be jus' as well off dead as not to have to have no more brains than me–I cain't figger out no way to git even with that big bully 'thout Junior to help. But iff'n I had the money I do b'lieve I'd buy me a pistol right now an' shoot him fulla bullets when he comes back. But he ain't a-carryin' my money with him, so I wouldn't git it back thataway . . . anyhow it don't do no good to figger when I ain't got no pistol an' cain't buy none. . . just supposin' this an' supposin' that is jus' nothin. . .

. . . Wonder iff'n he put it in another one o' them lockers? Iff'n he did I could watch an' when he's fixin' to git it I could bash his head in with somethin'. He's got it someplace, shore, an' I'm gonna hang onto him–he ain't about to git outta my sight from now on. . . . My belly's shore sore, I wish't I was twen'y years younger'n I am, we'd see. . . . I don'no what I can do by myself but looks as if I ain't gonna run inta Junior nor Donald so I might's well git on back down thataway.

Donald wouldn't be no help much anyhow, but I'd shore like to see Junior. He'd help me. He's smart, Junior is, an' can figger ways. . . . Wonder how smart that other feller is? How'd the polecat know my suitcase was packed with money? He might be 'most as smart as Junior–to figger that out like he done. . . .

My danged head's goin' around an' around, an' my nose is sore as a boil. My feet're killin' me. . . . Might's well git on down to the station an' set an' take a load off'n my feet for a spell. All I wanta do is not think no more. My nose is throbbin' like it was fulla Injuns beatin' tomtoms for a war dance. . . . I reely got trouble an' when I keep a-thinkin' about it all I just wanta cry . . . an' I cain't help it iff'n I'm cryin'. Let 'em look, dam' 'em–dam' ever'body anyhow! They don'no how bad I feel, an' I just cain't help it. . . .

CHAPTER NINE

JUNIOR KNOWLES

Over at the hotel, I punched the button to git the elevator 'fore I heard the hummin' that meant it was awready comin' down.

It stopped an' the door opened, an' a gal was standin' there in my way. She wasn't a bad looker an' I give her the once-over but I never got far as her legs—'cause at the end of her arm in a tight fist I seen the twin suitcase to mine! I knowed it had to be Donald's.

I taken a quick look behind an' seen the room clerk wasn't lookin' an' I hit that gal, hard, in the stummick. The air went outta her like a engine coughin' jes' as it runs outta gas. Time she hit the floor of the elevator, I was in an' had the door shet. I punched the button with the 3 on it an' it started up.

The gal was gittin' her breath but she was still green around the gills. I jerked her to her feet an' twisted her arm behind her back.

"Where's my brother—an' this here ain't no time to lie."

"He's asleep," she managed to git out.

She was bent over some, holdin' one hand tight ag'in her belly.

"Iff'n you done anything to him, I'm gonna kill you."

Up to now I hadn't got mad at nobody much. But now I was havin' to talk between my teeth, which was mashin' t' gether tight. So many folks buttin' in was gittin' on my nerves terrible bad. I knowed we was in a mess. All on account o' Donald never done like I told him. She wouldn't a-stole his suitcase 'thout knowin' what was inside. When the elevator come to a stop I slid the door open an' flung her out in the hall.

"Show him to me—fast!"

I give her arm a twist to show I meant bizness an' she pointed down the hall an' walked that way. She stopped an' I seen the number 303, like the bartender said. The door wasn't locked an' I shoved her halfway acrost the room in front o' me an' follered her in. I backhanded her once't acrost her thievin' little face, an' made her set down. Under all the warpaint I seen her skin was gittin' white.

"Scairt, ain'tcha? You got a right to be, woman."

Donald, he was sleepin' away on the bed. Naked an' real peaceful, like he musta been when all his money went for a walk in this gal's hands. Snorin' an' snortin', 'thout a worry in the wide world. The worryin' was all Junior's, looked as if.

I was mad enough to turn that bed over an' dump him on the floor, but I never. If somethin' ever happened to me I never knowed what in the world that kid'd do by hisself. Prob'ly git run over the first time he tried to cross the street.

I closed the door an' pushed the bolt, then I went over an' shaken him.

All I got was some groans and a louder snort than he'd been a-makin'.

I grabbed a glass settin' there an' filled it with water in the bathroom an' pulled Donald's face up from the pillow by the hair an' slammed the water in his face while I shaken him by the hair of his head. Might be painful but he'd brung it on hisself an' he hadta snap outta his dreams an' tell me what I hadta know.

62

Him an' the bed smelt like a moonshine dump with the still runnin' wide open. You coulda slapped likker outta the air with a paddle, it was so strong. He prob'ly wouldn't remember nothin'. His eyes begin 'comin' open a little an' I slapped him a couple times to help. He give me a stupid grin an' I hadta back outta the likker on his breath.

"Awright, fool," I said, "Git awake an' tell me what you been tellin' this here fancy gal."

He mumbled, but it wasn't words I could pick out. He started to lay back down, but I shaken him like playin' hully-gull with a double handful o' chinkapins.

"Git up an' git yore clo'es on."

He got off'n the bed an' near fell on his face, but he helt onta the bedstead an' started fumblin' with his clo'es. I wasn't goin' to help him 'cause I was so dam mad I coulda pinched his head off. I turned back to the gal while he put his clo'es on.

"Where'd he say he got the money?"

"What money?" she ast. Tryin' to lie to me when she knowed I knowed!

"You tryin' to tell me you ain't looked inta that there suitcase?"

"I was just taking it downstairs to check it for Donald and see if I could get him a room here, and—"

I smacked that gal so hard her teeth rattled an' blood started to run outta her mouth, an' I knowed the blood better be jes' in front of the truth. She started cryin' an' dam' if Donald didn't hit me in the back of my head with his fist! I had to take time to put him down, which wouldn't have been hard iff'n he'd a-been sober, much less drunked up like he was. I helt him with his arm behind his back.

"Awright, fool, now listen to me. This here gal was leavin' the hotel with yore suitcase when I caught onto her. Whatcha think she's dressed like she is for—she ain't figgerin' on nothin' but travelin' in that git-up. I know I'm doin' right an' you know I always know. What didja tell her 'bout our bizness?"

"I didn't tell nothin', Junior, honest."

He never looked me in the eye. He twisted his head an' looked at the wall while he was talkin'.

"Donald. Iff'n you wasn't my flesh-an'-blood brother I'd pull yore arm off at yore shoulder an' beat the truth outta you with the bloody end of it for sidin' with this here whore ag'in me. What didja tell her, I said?"

He never said nothin' but I got a answer, 'cause he kept his head down an' started to cryin'. The fool! It was plain he done told her ever'thing. He wasn't gonna git another drink long as he lived, or I'd whale the likker outen him with a treelimb.

"Git them bags. Quit squallin'. It don't help none. Git the bags like I say. Go to the elevator door an' *wait* on me. An' if you don't do like I say this time, Donald, I pity you, I shore do."

"You want me to take both bags, Junior?"

"Both bags. An' git goin'."

After he went I locked the door ag'in. Deeper an' deeper a man gits till. . . .

The gal was spittin' into a towel an' I seen she was missin' a tooth. Reckon she musta swallered it—I never seen it layin' around nowheres. She was cryin' hard. Who wouldn't, after comin' so close to bein' rich as she done an' havin' it jerked right outta their hands?

I knowed there wasn't nothin' I could git outta her I didn't awready know. She watched like a kid I used to know watchin' his mean stepdaddy. She looked so much like him I hadta laugh. It scairt her.

"What are you going to do?" she ast when I went tords her.

64

"Lay down on the floor–on yore belly."

She was scairt to an' scairt not to but scairter not to. She went down on her knees like a old cow an' then stretched her arms out, in a sorta crawlin' way, lookin' at me like maybe she was prayin'. Her eyes was all runnin' black from somethin' an' the cryin' had spread it all over her face. What with the way Donald couldn't be depended on to do nothin' right I never had no time to piddle none.

"I said, on yore belly!"

She went down flat then, an' tried to hide her face in the shaller rug. That was jes' right. The first time my blackjack smashed down on her head she quivered a little bit an' the cryin' stopped. I hit her time an' ag'in on the top of the head, up an' down, an' her head got softer an' softer.

I used the towel she'd been a-suckin' on an' wiped off my blackjack. I felt the big blood vessel in her neck with my finger an' couldn't feel it a-pumpin' no more so my worries about Donald's playmate was over. I stuck the blackjack in my pocket.

I taken a good look around the room to be shore Donald never left nothin' that'd be traced back to me an' him. Nothin' there so I picked up the doorkey layin' on the dressin' table an' locked the door behind me when I went out. It was a good thing for Donald he was waitin' on me like I told him.

"Did you do somethin' to Madge, Junior? Bad, I mean?"

"Shet yore trap!"

When the elevator stopped down at the bottom floor me an' Donald went th'oo the lobby an' out to the sidewalk. That room clerk never looked at us. Had his nose stuck in a funny-book so deep we coulda took all the furniture.

"Where we goin', Junior? I feel kinda sick."

"How'd you feel 'bout now iff'n I hadn't a-got yore money back?"

"Well, gee, Junior. . . . Maybe she was goin' to check it for me."

"You got a clod for a head? She was checkin' out with it."

I couldn't stay mad at Donald long. He never knowed no better. I shore worried about him, the li'l fool.

"I'm so tired, Junior. Where we goin'? Cain't we git a taxi?"

"The walk'll do you good. You'll git plenty o' ridin', 'cause we're goin' to the station an' you're catchin' the next bus to Oklahoma."

"I ain't goin', 'less you do."

"You ain't got nothin' to say 'bout it, Donald."

"I can get off the bus, first time it stops. I wanta stay with you, an' Leonie, when she comes."

"I cain't let you outta my sight fer five minutes 'thout you blabbin' ever'thing to somebody. I cain't watch you ever minute like a kid playin' with a straight razor. You got no bizness loose in a place like Big D."

"I didn't know I was a-sayin' all o' them things, Junior—hones' I didn't. I got drunk, an' Madge she got me all excited, an' thinkin' about that little gal a-callin' me Uncle Don an' ever'thing. I just didn't think, with all that there likker in me, Junior."

"That's jes' what I'm a-tellin' you, Donald. You shore never thought."

"Don't make me go back by m'self, Junior. . . . I promise, cross my heart an' hope to die I won't never drink no more likker."

I knowed he meant what he said when he was sayin' it, but they was no tellin' iff'n he'd remember it one day or three weeks. I'd just hafta watch clos'ter an' keep him with me all the time. I never reely wanted to send him back, 'cause I didn't like to think what not seein' that there kid would be like. We'd been a-walkin' all the time we was talkin' an' had come to the bus station.

"I'm goin' in here an' call Leonie on the phone, long distance. I'll see what she's got to say, an' maybe I won't send you home—I don't wanta make no promises about it."

"Can I talk to her too, Junior? Leonie likes me, an' she. . . ."

"We'll see."

I shoved the door open an' as we went inta the station dam' if I never seen ol' El Mercer settin' on a beach in the waitin' room. He was all bent over like a wearisome ol' man, a-holdin' his head in his hands. Maybe he was drunk, an' I never wanted to listen to him iff'n he was—I'd had me enough drunks for one day.

"Look, Junior! Yonder's El!"

"I ain't blind, Donald."

He went over tords where El was washin' his face in his dry hands. Hell with El. I went into a phone booth an' ast central to git me Sulphide, Oklahoma. I didn't even git her straight on what I was wantin' 'fore El come a-runnin' over tryin' to git in the booth with me. He was so danged excited I thought he was a-goin' to climb up on top an' try to come in through the roof.

"Goddammit, El! I'm a-tryin' to use the telephone!"

I had to put my hand in his face an' push his head outta the booth. He squealed like a stuck pig an' grabbed his nose with both hands.

Finally central was talkin' to Sulphide awright, an' then we had a hard time a-gittin' Leonie to the phone. Had to call Mrs. Allister an' ast her to go git Leonie, 'cause Leonie an' them never had no phone. An' all time I was waitin' El was actin' like he was goin' plumb slapdab crazy.

Outside the glass I could see him a-prancin' back an' forth an' actin' so anxious to talk to me it was as iff'n I was his best

gal or somethin'. He was makin' hurry-up signs an' beggin'
me to git through talkin'. I still wondered iff'n the ol' coot
was drunk.

I finally heard Leonie answerin' in Sulphide an' after a li'l
argyment with central I put in the handful o' change she said
it'd cost me to talk. Leonie was shore excited.

"Leonie, this's Junior . . . Shore is—I'm in Dallas—that's what
I'm a-phonin' you about . . . Naw, ain't a thing wrong . . .
Now looky here, s'pose you let me talk a minute an' I'll tell
you why I'm a-callin' . . . Dang it, I done toldja they ain't
nothin' wrong. I got a job . . . yeah, here in Dallas . . . What
kinda job? Oh, sellin' insurance . . . Now listen, Leonie, I
wantcha to catch a bus an' come down to Dallas right away—
soon's you can . . . I'll meetcha here at the bus station—nothin'
to be afeared of . . . Iff'n I ain't right in plain sight when you
git here, you jes' set an' wait a spell in the station 'til I show
up . . . An' Leonie, bring all yore clo'es, 'cause we're stayin'
. . . Shore we're gittin' married . . . Shore—plenty of money
. . . Naw, more'n thirty a week. They're payin' me thirty-five
. . . Okay, Leonie, honey, tomorrow mornin', then . . . Listen,
I gotta hang up now—this's costin' money . . . No, dammit, I
ain't drunk an' I'll meetcha . . . o' course I love you . . . I gotta
go now . . . Goodbye, Leonie."

I come outta that there booth sweatin' like a nigger at
election an' ol' El collared me. He was shootin' off his mouth
so fast I couldn't make no sense to what he said.

"Now, cool off, ol' man, an' tell me ag'in slow an' quiet—
who's been a-stickin' fingers in yore nose an' for what?"

When I begin to git it straight it was worse'n I'd thought.
Some guy had done stole ever penny of El's money, but he
wasn't satisfied—the crazy fool wanted to meet me an' Donald,
thinkin' he could steal our'n too. I was beginnin' to think a
man with money ain't got no friends a-tall.

'Fore El got through talkin' I never hadta guess none 'bout who the feller with the big idys was. Couldn't be nobody but the one settin' in El's car that very minute in fronta the house where I put him. I knowed I could see more trouble.

"El, you ol' fool! I swear I shoulda kept all yore money–an' yores too, Donald–an' only give it out to you one dollar at a time. I never seen folks so easy to take money away from a suitcase full at a time."

"Gawd–he never stole Donald's money, too, did he Junior?"

"Naw, not him. I hadta git his'n away from a gal what put him to sleep in her bed while she snuck out with it."

"I shore hope you can git mine back, Junior. Can you, Junior, huh, Junior?"

The li'l gal was out there in the car with this feller. When he got found he was gonna tell the cops about El. He knowed a whole sight more'n I figgered when I left him out there, 'cause El had spilt the beans. When the cops knowed about El it wouldn't take 'em long to latch onta him an' with a little slappin' around I knowed El would tell 'em all they wanted to know about me an' Donald. Then we'd all be a-danglin' from a cottonwood tree at the end of long ropes, likely.

Trouble was shore a-houndin' me, an' what hurt me so bad not none of it was of my makin'. But no matter who brung it on me, somethin' had to be did!

"What'd that there feller look like, El?"

"He's a big feller–'bout yay tall an' all man–an' he had black hair. Mostly what I 'member 'bout him is he kept a-grinnin' at me like a dam' skunk eatin' out of a hairbrush."

"That's the same feller, awright."

"You mean he's done been after you too, Junior?"

"I mean he prob'ly thought he was . . . El. Listen to what I'm a-sayin'. Me an' Donald, we got to go an' git him. I think

69

I can find him. You may as well know it, El–you done fixed it where I got to do a killin'.'"

"But he was doggone anxious to help me check my–"

"Shet up! That ain't helpin' to kill him. I'd make you do it, you ol' fool, iff'n I didn't figger you'd give him the clo'es you're wearin' an' maybe kill the wrong guy, b'sides."

"I'm sorry, Jun–"

"Dammit, shet up! An' jes' listen, like I say. Iff'n he ain't where he's s'posed to be I got to find him wherever he's at. You wait here. Iff'n I miss him an' he shows up to meetcha while me an' Donald's gone, you take him out to the fairgrounds. In 'at case, we'll meetcha out there an' I'll figger out what to with him then."

"Whereabouts at the fairgrounds you want him, Junior?"

Donald stuck his nose in about that time.

"Let's meet at that there Twirly-Whip," he said, an' I knowed the main thinkin' his head was able to do was how bad he wanted to git on that there twistin' ride ag'in. But I was all in a stew an' that was good as any place.

"That's where we'll meet, iff'n it works out he comes back here, El."

"S'pose he don't come back?"

"El, use yore head! Iff'n he don't you'll jes' be waitin' for him, wontcha? An' that's how I'll know where to find you ag'in iff'n he's out where I'm goin' now to look."

"Oh. Oh, yeah, I can see it now, Junior."

"The thing worryin' me ain't likely to enter yore head, El. That's iff'n he ain't where I'm goin' an' iff'n he don't come back to meet you, 'cause no matter where that feller's at we got to find him. I *mean* we got to. . . . C'mon, Donald."

My mind was havin' a reg'lar hissy inside my head. Donald gittin' drunk an' tellin' ever'thing, an' El tellin' ever'thing 'thout even gittin' drunk, an' me tryin' to git around everwheres fast enough to keep things all straightened out for the two dam' dumb fools. . . . I never hardly knowed which end was up. I was so tired I was plumb tuckered out an' they kept a-gittin' me in deeper all the time, an' there never seemed to be no end in sight.

All I knowed was that iff'n I couldn't figger out how to git it all to a stoppin' place somethin' terrible was gonna happen to all of us. An' it bein' me that planned ever'thing in the first place there jes' wasn't nothin' else to do but git it straightened out.

CHAPTER TEN

Bill Brown

I tried to turn my head before I was wide awake. It felt like somebody hitting ten thousand needles sticking in my scalp with a one-by-four plank.

A half-inch at a time I cranked my neck around to where I could get one hand up to the back of my head. I traced the outline of dried blood matted in my hair and was pretty sure someone had practiced on me with a sap.

I opened my eyes. The pain in them was a combination of Dengue Fever and a twenty-four hour stare at a live welding torch. No new blows came with my first movement so I became very brave and examined my surroundings. I had a lower berth—doubled up on the floorboards in the rear of an old sedan.

A bundle wrapped in a blanket was in the seat.

The blanket wasn't the best thing for concealing outlines, and with native curiosity egging me on I unrolled it to see who was keeping me company. With what I saw I was immediately able to identify myself as a most important cog in a kidnapping machine.

Disturbing the still figure as little as possible, I rolled the bundle back up.

Using the rest of my strength I raised the ball of lumps that was my head, until my eyes were on a level with the window. It seemed to be a quiet and peaceful neighborhood, with large lawns and large homes. The dirty rag on the floorboard was good for wiping the doorhandles when I got out.

I tried not to stagger; but so does a drunk, and I guess I was rolling worse than I thought. A sprinkler spraying away on the nearest lawn was beckoning, so I went that way. I shoved my head down into a cooling, misty nozzle. It brushed away cobwebs but it was no morphine for the pain. But it helped.

I had to find a phone book. I had to make a call, but it was the address I wanted. The call had to be in person. It was a miserable walk of two blocks before I found a drugstore. I went in.

"You got any bromo?" I asked the soda jerk.

"Yes, sir!""

"Keep 'em coming 'til I tell you to stop."

He was amazed but cooperative. After four sizzling glasses I held up my hand for the red light.

"What's the use?" I said.

"Hang a big one on, sir?"

"You could say that. Got a newspaper?"

He reached under the counter and came up with *The Morning News*. There it was, on the front page. I forced my aching eyes to focus:

HAAS CHILD BELIEVED DEAD!

Police Lieutenant Fred Campbell, in an interview with a *Morning News* reporter, stated, "We are doing everything possible, within the powers of the most modern crime detection section of any great city in the United States, to apprehend and bring to justice these nefarious and unscrupulous kidnappers. However, indications from certain sources which I cannot, for obvious reasons, reveal at this time, give us little hope that little Mary Ann Haas will be found alive."

What a jerk—but true to form of fumbling, explaining cops the world over. I read on.

Mr. Galin Haas, the broken-hearted father of little Mary Ann, would not admit reporters. According to a statement received from his oldest daughter, Miss Kay Haas, he is under the care of his private physician.

And Blah, Blah, Blah.

I looked up the broken-hearted father of little Mary Ann in the phone book and ordered another bromo at the fountain. I got it, together with several sympathetic waggles of the fountaineer's head.

"Where's this address, Buddy?" I shoved the piece of paper at him.

"Boy! You *must've* hung one on. That's right here in Highland Park—two blocks down to the left and you'll run into it."

73

"Thanks." I paid the jerk and left.

I walked, watching the numbers, and had no trouble finding the address. It was the house in front of which was parked an ancient LaSalle sedan, the same from which I had recently delivered myself.

The house was Texan colonial, brick, and had a movie-set driveway up to the wide front porch. I managed the driveway without crumpling with awe, and pushed a button that chimed out deep inside the mansion. I wasn't sure I wanted that door to open. But it did.

The woman who opened it looked at me with eyes that tried to duplicate the cooling nozzle I'd drenched my head in. But the rest of her made liars out of the cold eyes. The most perfunctory glance couldn't have missed the warmth of sex oozing from her fulsome figure like milk from a discarded can.

"Bill Brown," I explained.

"Reporter?" She got ready to slam the door between us.

"Uh-uh. But I know where Mary Ann is. You'd never guess where."

I don't know what reaction I was waiting for. Regardless, I could still be waiting—none came.

"Come in."

I followed her down a hallway lined by a photo-mural of an oil field in full production. It was bathed in indirect light, and I thought it must be symbolic advertising in their small way of where wealth comes from in a big way.

"In here," she said.

I mentally tallied the words she had spoken since opening the door. Five. And she knew I probably had answers to any number of questions she should be asking. I decided she had better control over curiosity than cats and women.

The door she led me through brought us into a library too large to be called a room. Two walls were books, a third was an enormous photo in full color of a single steel derrick standing in a barren area of sagebrush and mesquite. The last wall was all window, facing a garden colored by somebody like Bonnard.

Galin Haas was sitting facing the window-wall, staring at the garden. He was so lost in thought he didn't hear us come in.

"Dad," she said, "this is Mr. Brown, and he has news about Mary Ann."

I was surprised that it penetrated his coma-like appearance, but he turned his head toward me. His eyes belonged to a dog that gets a daily beating, is due for that beating, and knows he must take it. I felt like my toenails were snarled in a wool blanket.

"Mr. Haas, I'd like to soften this but I don't know how. Your daughter is dead. Do you want me to bring her in?"

The girl's reaction was pantherish.

"You son of a bitch! Why didn't you tell *me* she was dead?"

"You didn't ask."

Mr. Haas had turned back to the garden and I waited for something to come from him.

"Bring her in, please, Mr. Brown," he said softly.

I must have hesitated.

"Bring her in! You heard what he said."

I shrugged and walked out through the oil field in the hall to the door. I turned and started back to the library, and she was standing in the doorway watching me in a detached manner. "Something wrong, Mr. Brown?"

"I won't answer that—not now. But I thought it might be better if I drove around to the back."

"All right. I'll open the back door for you."

"Thanks."

A ringless, companionless key was sticking in the ignition lock. The old engine jumped to life and was surprisingly smooth as I swung into the drive and turned off where the gravel entered a loop that circled toward the rear of the house.

She opened the door just as I reached it with the blanket load of murdered girl, and led me through the house to the library.

"Over there."

She pointed and I laid the dead child on a kidney-shaped desk. I was beginning to get sore. What the hell kind of people were these stoics, anyhow? Well, if they could be hard, I could be blunt. No use using a fishing pole for a battering ram.

"Look," I said. "What I have seen shows me you wouldn't be greatly disturbed if you don't get your fifteen thousand dollars back. But—if you're interested in putting a loop on the kidnappers, I'm it. I also come high."

"We are."

That's all she said. No encouragement, no objection. So I went on, feeling my way through the look in her eyes.

"This is immaterial, but, in addition to being an expensive employee, I'm wanted by the police."

"As a kidnapper, naturally," she said calmly.

"You'll have to take my word I'm not one of 'em. It's entirely possible some people would disagree with me at this stage of the game."

"As you said, that's immaterial. If you're one of that rotten gang and I can buy the others from you, I'll be that far ahead."

"I have one idea—with two angles, Miss Haas. The idea is to work on this gang and smear them. The angles—personal interest and financial gain."

"The best men in town are working on it already."

"Yeah—I read his sage remarks in the newspaper."

"I don't mean the police."

"I see what you do mean. Pull 'em off—now. There's no opening in this job for smart sleuthing of the private boys. It'll cost you good money to get perfect alibis of known Dallas hoodlums and dopeheads. None of 'em did it. Unless by a million-to-one stumble-bum chance one of these dumb kidnappers does something logical, nobody but me can touch 'em."

"I'll take that chance."

"Then you don't hire me. I don't want any bright boys trailing me around when I leave here. Call 'em off, or you lose your bet."

She looked at me for a long time.

"There's another thing," she said. "We want them before the police get them. If you think you can deliver, I may hire you."

"I think I can."

"What do you think, Dad?"

"Pay him. Have him bring 'em here."

He kept looking without looking at the garden.

"Five hundred will do for a retainer," I told her, "and for each one delivered a bonus of five hundred more."

The old man had been listening. He spoke up again.

"The bonus will be one thousand apiece, if they are alive when you bring 'em in."

"That's fair."

Miss Haas sat at the desk and started to fill in a check.

"Cash, if you don't mind."

She took ten bills from a purse on a nearby table and handed them to me.

"Make the call," I said.

"What call?"

"The one that pulls the private eyes off my back."

It only took a minute, though she probably ran into objections from the other end of the wire. She simply informed them the gravy train was pulling into a siding as of that minute. If I know private detectives their interest died awfully fast.

"Satisfied?" she asked.

"I'll need a gun."

She dug in the purse again and brought out a toy pearl-handled .25 and held this bit of lethal artillery out to me. I shook my head.

"I said, I'll need a gun."

She shrugged, pulled a drawer of the desk open and handed me an Army .45.

"I'll need a change of clothes."

She left the room and I went along behind and up the sweeping staircase, with my eyes as wide as the pain would allow. What a woman!

I guess the room we went into was her father's bedroom. She slid open the wardrobe and pointed carelessly at the long rack of clothes. She stood watching me, and I waited. She kept watching. It was confusing, and I wondered what she'd do if I started peeling down. But it was bad enough just being in a room that held both this woman and a bed—without taking any further risks.

"I'll be down as soon as I change."

I couldn't tell if the eyes held scorn or not as she turned away. I felt like they did, though, which was just as bad. She left.

Mr. Haas had class. Being closer to thirty-eight than thirty-two around the centerline, I had to play a lot of hide-and-seek before I found anything to wear. The only suit I could get into that fit halfway decently was a tweed—and I suspected Mr. Haas had seen more portly days and the tweed must have been a reminder.

Tweed, in Dallas in the middle of summer. Well, I couldn't wear that rag Ed had brought me any longer. I picked a white nylon sport shirt without tie, argyle socks, and was a little happier when the shoes were right and I could take a pair of suede sandals. My feet would be cool, at least. I went down-stairs.

She was waiting, with her deadpan expression.

"I've decided to go with you."

"No. The party may be rough. Some other night, maybe?"

Her eyes, strong enough to feel, bored into my back from the doorway as I walked down the drive to the street. Two blocks down I found a bus stop and waited. I stepped into the first one. I had taken off the coat and wished I could do the same with the pants.

When I got downtown I walked to the bus station, realizing I still had no plan of action. The air conditioning inside was like lemon juice running through chipped ice and I thought how well I'd like to spend the rest of my life right there.

I found my man, looking at a much-thumbed comic book he'd probably scavenged out of a waste pile. An intense frown separated his yellow eyes above the red nose, and his lips moved slowly as he struggled with the printed word.

I aimed a brisk kick at his shin. It landed and he leaped to his feet—or one foot, rather. He was holding the shin I bruised and doing an odd sort of dance.

"Where are they?" I asked him.

"Dangit, dangit, dangit! You done skint all the hide off'n my laig! What'n thunderation's eatin' on you, Mister?"

"Let's talk some business."

"Heck of a way to start a talk—tryin' to break a man's laig. Now, wait a minute!"

I'd made a slight feint and he nearly fainted.

"They're gonna meet us, awright. I had a hard time a-findin' 'em, but I toldja I would. Only thing, Junior, he wouldn't meetcha in town an' they're waitin' on us out at the fairgrounds."

"Good. Where, at the fairgrounds?"

"They'll be by the Twirly Whup. That's a ride. It goes. . . ." and he described it with some crazy hand waving. From his description I didn't think I'd care to ride it.

"Okay, We'll take a cab."

We walked out and I opened the door of the first taxi in the line.

"Fairgrounds," I said.

The cab jerked away from the curb, and I took a look at the driver. Another woman hackie. . . .

CHAPTER ELEVEN

KAY HAAS

Dad didn't know what Lieutenant Fred Campbell had told me—that a Bill Brown had escaped from a hotel downtown and Dad's suitcase with part of the ransom was found in his room.

I'd kept it from Dad because I didn't want him to know the kidnappers had already divided the money and separated. I thought I knew what that meant, and Dad was upset too much already.

Now what? I'd handed a Bill Brown five hundred dollars, a hundred dollars worth of clothing and a gun to kill somebody else with. And then I let him walk out of the front door like he owned the town. I had even taken our detectives off his trail—that is, if they could find a trail without painted arrows to point the way.

Now I wished I had told Dad. He wouldn't have been easy.

That name, Bill Brown. Knowing he'd had that money. How in the world had I believed he wasn't one of them? Well, did I believe he wasn't? Here I stood like a damned fool waiting for him to turn his best friends over to me. If they all got away together now I'd be real proud of myself. Especially if someone got killed with the gun I gave him.

If Bill Brown was a fake name—like Fred Campbell said—why would he use it here, knowing the police had it from the hotel register? He didn't look stupid, whatever else he was.

Wouldn't he just pick another name to give me? Or did he just not give a damn? He'd had that look about him, all right.

To come here of all places, without even a gun, and say "I'm Bill Brown"! Simpler to go to the police and ask for a sheet of paper to write his confession on. Why did he bring Mary Ann home . . . why care if we never found her? Conscience? I didn't think so.

I was finally coming face to face with myself. I had trusted him—hadn't really believed he was one of them. My heart still didn't think so. But I was so afraid now that my heart was doing my thinking instead of my brain. Something about that bruiser my heart had trusted while my head tried to warn me.

He'd looked like a wrestler with slightly hunched shoulders. But his face had been kind—almost a little handsome, in a rugged way. His eyes seemed to brim with pain and trouble, but he hadn't complained. Just laid his cards on the table—and I wished I knew whether or not he dealt them from the bottom of the pack. He was a complete contrast to the men I see very much of. Was that the trouble? That I'd met a *man*, whether crooked or honest? Had it spoiled my judgment? Hell, I didn't know.

I went back to the library and slumped on the arm of Dad's chair. I smoothed his hair with one hand while I talked.

"Would you want to take a look at Mary Ann, Dad?"

"Not yet, Kay. . . . Do you remember what I did with that bull-whip? The one I had made at the ranch?"

"I can find it, Dad. . . . But Dad, there's something I want to talk about."

I broke down and told him the whole story. He was quiet when I finished. I waited, knowing he was looking at it as I had—trying to read this Bill Brown from what he now knew. He stirred and took a deep breath through open lips.

"Well, Kay—there's no way to be sure, is there?"

"If I've done wrong I'll never forgive myself."

"Forgive yourself? You've no cause for that sort of talk—none a-tall."

"Do you think I should put the detectives back on the job? And tell the police?"

"No. Neither bunch could find the Magnolia Building if you turned the lights off the flying horse on top. We'll wait a while."

"I'm glad you said that, Dad. I want to hope this Brown is on the square—till we know I'm wrong, anyhow."

"Kay . . . it's hard, this loss. I . . . never should have moved you all to town. One of the ranches was the place for us. But I wanted bigger and better things for you all, I guess. . . ."

" Dad! Don't say things like that—hush!"

"Kay, I—"

I interrupted him. We were both close to the breaking point.

"Never mind—I've lots to do now, Dad. I'm going to call Lieutenant Campbell, first."

I dialed headquarters. It was a good thing I didn't need him in a hurry. Having to wait so long gave me more determination to throw him off the track. He finally answered.

"Lieutenant, Mary Ann is home," I told him. "Yes, they did . . . the worst . . . Some man brought her in . . . No, he didn't give his name. I was under great shock, naturally. And I gave him a reward . . . five hundred . . . I don't know—he left here walking, I think. I can't remember very . . . Well, he said he wasn't interested in publicity . . . Hold him? Now, Lieutenant, how could I hold him? . . . I couldn't say, of course, but I don't think so—he said he wasn't one of them. No, I'm afraid I couldn't even describe him. He was here just a few minutes, and under the circumstances I just . . . Yes . . . Yes . . . Yes, of course I realize now if we had cooperated with you sooner things might be different, but . . . sorry, that's the best I can do—won't you try to put yourself in my place . . . Really, Lieutenant, this isn't getting us very far and I feel so little like talking at all . . . You know it's hard for me to talk of it, even to you; but I felt it was a duty that couldn't . . . I'm awfully sorry, I must go—I've so much to do now, and these next hours will be very difficult for us, so if you don't mind . . . Goodbye, Lieutenant."

My report hadn't been all lies, at any rate. When Martha Jane had phoned from the fair that she had lost Mary Ann I'd told her not to come back to the house. And knowing Dad's temper I'd sent the rest of the servants home, too. Dad was wonderful to his family, always; but he was a cold, brittle sample of holy terror when he was in a rage.

I couldn't understand how in the world Martha Jane had lost Mary Ann in broad daylight. Negro-like, she'd been so scared she had cried and moaned and screamed into the phone so I couldn't get any idea of what had happened, except that Mary Ann was lost.

But somebody was going to pay for this rotten deal. If I had to spend every oil well and every head of cattle we owned. Whoever paid wouldn't enjoy the method of collection, either. In years on a ranch I've never seen anyone as deadly with a bull-whip as Dad. I saw him prove it on a cowboy once when I was about sixteen.

The hand had let his romance turn from guitar strumming to mauling me around quite a bit before I got away from him and went tearing into the ranch house crying and yelping, with the denim shirt I'd had on trailing mostly behind me. The boys caught him before he got to the border and brought him back days later.

Dad had been judge and jury, and the punishment he dealt out with his whip still makes me shudder to think of it.

But I knew I could thrill to the sight of these kidnappers getting within the terrible slashing strokes of Dad's whip. I went to the closet off the back hall and got the whip and took it to him. He fondled the heavy handle absently, his eyes smoldering with hate and hope. With the barest suggestion of motion he flicked the long lash across the room into the corner like a striking snake. It was uncanny, his easy command of that writhing, searching coil.

"Thank you, Kay—feels good in my hand again. . . . Will you take care of the funeral arrangements, and call everybody that should know, and—"

"Don't worry, Dad. I'll take care of things."

"I hate to ask you to shoulder these burdens, but. . . ."

"Don't fret, Dad. We'll find those men sooner or later, and when we do I'll get as much satisfaction from it as you do."

His thoughts had taken over and he didn't answer me. I went to my room to spare him the details of the phone calls I'd have to make.

The undertaker was prompt in coming, and left with Mary Ann. Except for insisting on an evening funeral, which he objected to, I left most of the details up to him. A blunt reminder that it was my grief, my wish, and my money he was arguing with erased his objections.

I called the newspapers and gave them bare essentials. They would distort everything anyhow, so the less they had to work on the less they could sensationalize. They didn't seem satisfied with what they got, but I simply hung up when they had what I'd decided to give them.

At last I was through. I soon began to feel lost in the reaction of having nothing else to busy myself with.

I showered and changed into a tailored linen suit just to kill time and cool off.

I went down to the kitchen and browsed around, trying to think of something real nice to fix for Dad. I fixed a bowl of broth and took it to him. He thanked me but he didn't want it, and as I threw it out I wondered if he even knew I had offered it to him.

I ate a banana. Then I perked some coffee and drank a few swallows and poured most of it in the sink, and went back up to my room.

The inactivity was maddening. It didn't seem like Dad would stir for hours yet. I read the first sentence four times in a book I picked up, so I threw it across the room. I was listening for something–and the something was the chimes that would tell me Bill Brown was at the door again. I tried to keep them from it, but my thoughts kept coming back to him and wondering what he was doing.

I went back downstairs and Dad hadn't moved, but the tip of the lash was in a different corner now. I tried to think of more phone calls I should make. No one I wanted to talk to came to mind except Bill Brown. I opened the front door, looked out, and closed it again. Then I fixed a drink but it didn't have any taste. Not a sound in the house. I started back to my room but I changed my mind because I knew there was nothing in there I hadn't picked up and put down a dozen times already,

I finally sat down on the bottom step of the stairs. I looked at the wall till I couldn't see it; then at the front door. Something hurt me, and I found I was almost biting through my lower lip. I thought of Mother and was glad she wasn't alive to know about things. I thought of Mary Ann and the way she'd looked in her little red suit, and how happy she was when she left to go to the fair. I couldn't take it.

I began to cry.

CHAPTER TWELVE

DONALD KNOWLES

I didn't know what got Junior inta such a big hurry when we started outta the bus station, but he shore was.

I was half-runnin' to stay up with his long legs. He hollered at a taxi an' when it stopped we got in. I lean't back, hopin' whatever come off it'd work out so's we could git out to the fairgrounds ag'in. The driver ast us for a address but Junior wouldn't tell him none.

"Jes' you start drivin'," he said, "straight down this here street an' take the turns I tellya. Thataway we'll git where I'm hankerin' to go."

The driver moved his shoulders up an' down like it didn't make him no differ'nce, an' done like Junior said. Junior give him the turns to make as we went. I didn't even watch where we was goin'–I didn't know an' didn't care. So I just had a good time ridin'.

All of a sudden Junior told the driver to stop at a drugstore we was 'bout to pass. He paid him an' waited till he drove off an' turned back tords town. We was in a purty place.

All the streets was curved in long curves like a race track, an' the houses was set 'way back in big green yards. All the grass was cut, smooth as a billiard ball. I didn't get too much time to look.

"C'mon," Junior sorta barked it at me.

"Walk, Junior?"

"I said c'mon—you comin'?"

"Well, sure, Junior, but we had us a good ride. Now we got to walk?"

"Walk."

"How far we gotta walk?"

"Iff'n you an' old El could ast as many questions afore you git in trouble as you do when I'm a-tryin' to straighten it out, we wouldn't be out here. We gotta walk about two blocks. That ain't no trouble—the trouble's at the end of the walk."

We started down the street an' walked one block an' 'bout half of another one. Junior stopped an' I bumped into him. He was lookin' straight down the street with a frown on his face I didn't like none too much.

"You see El's old LeSalle anywheres, Donald?"

I looked ever' whichaway but there wasn't no cars on the street nowheres.

"Naw, I cain't see it nowheres. Where's it at?"

"That's jest it. It was right in fronta that there big house. The one with them big white porch poles."

"Well, you can see it ain't there, Junior, 'thout astin' me. Does it matter?"

Junior looked mad enough to bite ten-penny nails apart, an' kinda s'prised, too. He was swearin' a steady stream. He whirled around an' started walkin' back tords the drug store. I didn't useta mind walkin' so bad back in Oklahoma, but I was sure beginnin' to like ridin' in taxis since we had money, an' all this walkin' was tirin' me out.

"We shoulda kept the taxi," Junior told me. "Now we gotta catch a bus back downtown."

Heck, I'd wanted to keep it all the time, but I was scared to say so now. We waited a few minutes at the corner by the drugstore an' a bus come along goin' tords town. It stopped an' we got on. Junior was so quiet it didn't seem like him. He

88

was worried, 'cause I could see big frowny-lines between his eyes. I couldn't figger out why, but I guessed it was part my fault.

I wished I could tell him I was sorry for bein' such a danged fool with Madge an' purt-nigh losin' my money to her. But I wasn't sure if it'd make him feel better, or make him mad to remind him of her again. It ain't good to bother my brother when he's so quiet, so I decided ag'in sayin' anything.

Me an' El had shore got him in a lot of trouble, an' by now he musta been purty tired of tryin' to keep us outta hot water all the time. Looks like me bein' his brother he woulda told me what we was goin' to do. But he didn't say nothin' a-tall an' I kept my mouth shut an' waited. First thing I know we was back downtown ag'in.

Junior yanked on the cord which buzzes the thing up by the driver that you want off. When we was off he got us another taxi an' this time he told the driver where to take us.

"Bus station."

"Which one, Buddy?"

"That one next to the newspaper buildin'–an' don't buddy me. I ain't got no buddies in this here town."

"Awright, awright!"

At the bus station Junior paid him an' give him a hard look; then we went in the station. He looked over where we left El a-waitin' for the man they was talkin' about. El wasn't there. I follered Junior while he walked all through the station. No El nowhere.

"C'mon," Junior told me.

Outside the station he took the first taxi. I was gettin' happy ag'in, with him grabbin' taxis ever' time he got near one. Shore makes a difference when you get useta havin' money, an' I snuggled my bag up closer. I was happier yet when he told this driver where we was goin'.

"Fairgrounds–the shortest way."

It was gettin' dark, an' I was thinkin' how purty the fair would be all lit up.

Junior seemed a little happier, too. Reckon he was glad he didn't find El. That meant that feller had come back to meet El an' El musta carried him to the Twirly Whip to wait for Junior an' me.

When the driver got us to the fairgrounds Junior had him go in an' drive around, tellin' him how to go. He was getting' away from the brightest parts, away from the purty midway. In a minute or two he musta saw what he wanted, 'cause he told the driver to circle back on the street we had just come down.

"We'll git out by that there Opera House."

"I think that one's closed, Mister. The open-air house is . . "

"Iff'n you want to git paid, stop yore taxi where I tellya!" Junior said. He shore was touchy.

The driver wanted to git paid an' he let us out by the place Junior said.

I'd rather a-got out where I could git a hot dog an' ride the Twirly Whip, but Junior feelin' like he was I wasn't doin' none of my thinkin' out loud. He paid the driver an' turned to me, takin' holt of my arm.

"Donald, this here's a Opera House an' its closed up. Nobody 'round here a-tall. Right over yonder is some trees. See? It's good an' dark over there. That's the place we wanta end up with that feller who stole El's money an' thinks he wants our'n too. 'Member this spot. I gotta figger some way to git him down here."

"Well, cain't we go on over to the midway? We can get us a hotdog, first, huh? Then we can go see if El's got the feller where he's s'posed to meet us."

"Ain't no time for no hot dawgs! We're goin' straight to the Twirly Whup." He started walkin' but he didn't cut over to the midway. Just went right up the street we was awready on. We went past a place that was just a big high fence all around 'cept where the ticket window was. I could hear music comin' over the sides, with singin', an' it sure sounded nice a-floatin' out into the warm air. I woulda liked to a-gone in an' seen it.

"This must be the open air place the taxi man was talkin' about," I told Junior.

The sign out in front of it said "SHOWBOAT–Last Operetta of the Season." Junior just grunted an' turned off to cut acrost the grass tords the midway.

We kept outta sight when we got purty close, an' moved up behind a hotdog stand where we could see acrost to the Twirly Whup. The smell of them hotdogs was about drivin' me wild, I was so hungry for one. But I seen what Junior'd awready saw–El was standin' over there with a big man in a white shirt.

The feller with El was a-rubbin' the sides of his head with his fingers an' ever' little bit he'd say somethin' to El. He looked mean enough to hunt bear with a switch. Ever' time he turned to look at El it looked as if El was gonna run for the gates. He was scared, I figgered.

I wasn't scared none. The feller wasn't much bigger than Junior an' the way my brother was feelin', I knew it was just too bad for anybody he was mad at. I reckoned the feller in the white shirt was about as mean as he looked, awright, to jam his fingers in El's nose. First time I ever heard of that. But he shoulda seen Junior the time I seen him hit a big guy in Oklahoma in the belly with a baseball bat an' then stompin' up an' down on him while he was layin' on the ground tryin' to git his breath. The man with El would have to go some to

91

be as mean as Junior when he was mad. An' right now Junior was awful, awful quiet.

"Come back here, Donald!"

That was the first I knew my nose had been a-pullin' me around tords the hot dog counter. Junior yanked me back of the buildin' outta sight.

"Listen to me, now, an' fergit them dam' hot dawgs till we git this here mess cleaned up!"

"Awright, Junior. What'll I do?"

"Jes' what I tellya. Listen. I'm goin' back down the street inta them trees I showed you back of the Opera House—the closed one. You gotta give me five-six minutes to git set. Then you go on over to El an' this stranger an' tell 'em I'm ready to talk but I don't wanta git out in the lights."

"Okay, Junior."

"That ain't all—keep listenin'. You lead 'em down to where I'm at. When y'all git there we'll start talkin', an' I'll give a signal, like scratchin' my head. We'll all pile on that feller an' git him down. When he's down I'll fix his clock—with my blackjack so's it won't make no noise. Now, you got it straight?"

I nodded my head.

"How straight? Tell it back to me."

I did, just like he told it to me. He was satisfied then, an' he lit a shuck down tords them trees.

Six minutes, he said, so I know I had time enough to git a hotdog. I got one an' put a lot of mustard on it to make it twice't as good. Then I started acrost to where El was a-waitin', eatin' my dog an' watchin' that big feller.

"Hi, El," I said.

I didn't like the way the stranger looked at me. Looked like he didn't like me too much, neither. Nor nobody.

"You're not Junior the Brain, are you?" he ast.

"Shucks, no, Mister—I'm just Donald."

El looked mighty worried. The big guy swung around tords him, an' El throwed his hands up between 'em.

"Hold yore hosses, now, Mister," he said, "till I find out where Junior went."

"Thirty seconds. After that you won't be able to hear what happened to Junior—you'll be wondering what else can happen to you."

"Donald, wh—where is Junior?" El was whinin' like a old hound dog after he's got caught chasin' chickens. "Tell him, Donald, quick—where is Junior? This feller ain't got no pity on nobody. Tell him, won'tcha hurry up an' tell him?"

"Shore, El." I looked at the big guy an' laughed. "You may not be so happy to see him, Mister."

Next thing I know my hot dog was squashed flat, all over my face. Mustard squirted ever'wheres—in my eyes an' on my new clo'es, an' it stung my eyes worse'n onion juice. I sputtered an' wiped, an' tears was runnin' outta my eyes, an' I backed away from him. El caught me an' helped me—taken my hankachief outta my hip pocket an' helped me. When I could see ag'in I found some of the mustard on my bag an' started to cleanin' it off. El done it for me, talkin' all the time.

"Donald, for Gawd's sake tell the man what he wants to know, son! He's the meanest one man I ever seen. Don't rub him the wrong way—he'll do no tellin' what to both of us."

I figgered El was prob'ly right.

"Junior's waitin' for us, Mister. He told me to tell you he'd listen to what you got to say. He sent me after you an' El."

"That's better. Where?"

He was a-blinkin' at me like a old owl in the sunshine. Like his eyes was hurtin' bad as mine with the mustard in 'em. I thought maybe he was goin' crazy. Musta been, thinkin' he was gonna take Junior's money. I stayed away from him. No tellin' what a man like that's gonna do next, an' I'd done made him mad once't.

"I'll show you. You gotta go with me to where he is."

"We're wasting time, Donald, my boy. You two go in front and I'll tag along behind."

So I started off, goin' behind the hot dog stand. Them hot-dogs didn't smell good a-tall no more. I figgered it'd be a spell 'fore I'd eat another hotdog.

I cut acrost the grass, with El walkin' beside me.

"Where's Junior at?" he ast.

I looked over my shoulder, but the mean guy was about fifteen yards back.

"He's down yonder in some trees by the opera house."

I hadn't no more'n got the words outta my mouth when my bag of money tore right outta my hand!

I hollered, an' I seen the big guy an' his white shirt hotfootin' it acrost the street to the ticket window at that open-air place! He was buyin' a ticket just as cool as you please. After stealin' my bag with all my money! I hollered at him ag'in an' started after him, El right beside me. The feller had got a ticket an' was goin' up them steps about six at a time. I had to get a ticket too, or I wouldn't get in to catch him. I shoved El to one side an' went tords the ticket window.

"Don't foller me, El, you crazy fool! Go down yonder an' get Junior!"

El turned an' started runnin' tords the place where Junior was s'posed to be at, an' I bought a ticket.

"I wanta sit alongside o' that feller that just got a ticket," I said. "He's a uncle of mine."

She give me one an' I had to pay full price for it. I knew the show had been goin' on awhile an' I wouldn't git to see it all, but there wasn't no time to argy so I give her the money.

I went on in, an' couldn't see the feller with my bag. I was still lookin' around for him when a girl come up an' taken my ticket. She led me with a little flashlight to where my seat was an' pointed to it. Sure 'nough, the big stranger was settin' there next to me.

He didn't seem a-tall s'prised when I set down. Just kept a-watchin' the show, like he was a honest man an' had been there all the time, the big thief! I reached for my bag an' he slapped my hand. He moved the bag over on the other side of him an' started watchin' the show ag'in.

"You gimmie that bag!" I said to him.

He didn't answer me, but a old biddy settin' in back of me shushed me, right in the ear, "Sh-h-h!"

I shushed for a second, but I wanted that bag—awful bad, same as anybody woulda. I was goin' crazy wantin' to get my hands on it ag'in.

"Mister, that's my bag you got there," I whispered.

He turned his head just a little bit an' said "Sh-h-h-sh!" so loud I jumped myself. An' the man in fronta me turned around an' give me a terrible dirty look. I felt like cryin', it all made me so mad. They both turned back to watch the stage an' I could see there wasn't no use tryin'. He wasn't gonna give it back by me just astin' for it. An if I didn't keep shut the people would have me throwed out for botherin' 'em, an' that was what he was after, I figgered. A few of the people's heads kept turnin' to me like they was just a-waitin' for one more peep outta me, so what could I do?

I just lean't back an' watched the stage myself. This had cost me money, after all, an' I could depend on Junior to take care of the man with my bag later. All I had to do was set tight an' watch him an' keep close to him, an' wait for Junior to come.

He'd make this big bully sorry he ever seen Dallas!

95

CHAPTER THIRTEEN

BILL BROWN

The lights were bright on the Midway.

A poor man's Santa Monica—everything except ocean and cool breeze. The roar of the damned Twirly Whip magnified the pain in my head while I watched the stupid people passing by.

These Dallasites worked at being a cosmopolitan clan. The women were all fully dressed, most of them all the way to hats and gloves, instead of the sensible shorts of the California female bent on outdoor recreation in town or country. Stupid.

Sweat. Running down my face, down my back. Gradually saturating the twigs in the tweed of my trousers. Under my shirt the gun was sticky against my stomach. The heavy English tweed jacket lolled across my arm like a passed-out drunk. I was sick of waiting, but I still couldn't think what to do if and when the other two kidnappers did show.

I gave the old man a hard time.

"Pop." He ducked. "What makes your nose so big?"

"You hadn't oughtta josh me 'bout my nose, not after what you done to it. It's ahurtin' me som'p'm awful."

"If those two don't show in about five more minutes it'll hurt you a lot more."

"Now, jest a minute, Mister. 'Tain't my fault iff'n they ain't here in five minutes. Junior said he'd come an' he'll be here, awright, but he never said jes' when."

"I said when. Five minutes—then nose, look out!"

It worried him. Well, I was worried and felt like passing some of it along. Misery loves company. Brown, you're a mean man, I thought. I tried to shift the pain about by twirling my temples with my fingers.

Then a kid coming toward us was giving me a close inspection. In one hand was a leather bag and in the other a foot-long hotdog which was dripping mustard into his sleeve. From his wary eyes I pegged him for one of the covey I was gunning for. If my guess was right I could go further and picture the leather bag lined with folding stuff. He looked a little under the weather. His face was pasty white with sprinkled-paprika cheeks, and his eyes were two blood-covered lemon drops. Like he might have been celebrating his recent financial success with bottled elation.

A couple of questions established that he wasn't Junior the ringleader. So this was Donald.

"Then where is Junior?" I said.

He cracked wise and I smashed the hotdog into his face. He was glad to talk then and offered to lead me to Junior. I made him and the whining old man go in front and I followed.

They went across the Midway, crossed a strip of lawn between it and the next street, and turned down to the left. My scrambled brain was beginning to grind out a glimmer of a plan. We were approaching the summer operetta amphitheatre. The plan crystallized.

I swooped to the left of young Donald, gathered his bag into my hand, and double-timed across the street. At the ticket window I slapped down a five-dollar bill.

"One, please," I said.

She had one, and with it I bounded up the steps and into the darkness around the audience. An usherette took me to the quickly-purchased seat and left me with the rumbling bass notes and voices of "Old Man River" to vie with the rest of the pains in my head.

I sat quietly–giving my mind time to give birth to another brilliant idea. I hoped the next one would counteract the one that had fenced me in. Brilliance wasn't needed to realize the exits to this place would be sealed tighter than King Tut's tomb as soon as Junior arrived to help. I wondered if I had guessed right about the contents of the bag. I got my answer to that.

The usherette brought Donald over and put him in the seat next to mine. Nothing would persuade him to be that reckless except his part of those ill-gotten greenbacks, I felt sure. He was worried. I didn't look at him, but kept my eyes on the performance down front. He reached for the bag and I rapped his hand and pushed it away.

"Sh-h-h-sh!"

He soon gave up, got quiet, and became interested in the show.

The old man playing the part of the blustering Captain was good. I wanted to enjoy it myself but there was too much mental distraction. I kept wishing I was on a showboat on the Mississippi myself, pulling into New Orleans–maybe with a plane waiting. . . . But that wasn't getting me anywhere.

I got up and squeezed past the kid.

"Excuse me," I said.

Oddly enough, he followed. I paused at the refreshment stand for a coke to wash down a couple of headache powders, and wondered how long it had been since that gorgeous cashier had told me to hurry back. I looked, and hadn't lost Donald. But he wasn't getting too close.

I thought a side exit would be the best choice, and dodged through one out into the street. He followed along–still not close enough for me to grab.

I went back the way we came in a hurry, expecting something unpleasant every step—such as a bullet in the back or a flying tackle. Nothing happened.

I found traffic, and in the traffic I found a cab. It stopped and backed up when I whistled.

"Where to?"

"Wait just a minute. I'll have company, I think. Keep the engine running."

I left the door open and didn't even look out the window. It didn't take over a minute. Donald stuck his head in the door.

"Where you goin' with my suitcase?"

"Want to find out?"

He hesitated. I could read the indecision in his face as if it had been typewritten. What would happen to him if his brother found out that I had got away from him, and if I did get away how would he ever see the money again? It turned out he was either less afraid of me than of Junior or the money was a powerful magnet. He got in the cab, scrambling to the far corner of the seat. His eyes were as wide as a double door.

"Highland Park," I said to the driver.

He moved out, professionally, like any good male cabby anywhere.

Chapter Fourteen

Kay Haas

I kept trying hard to cry but finally no more tears would come.

That made the aching worse. My lungs felt dry and stuffy and the tightness in my throat hurt because I couldn't release it any longer. The tears had helped before; now I couldn't get my breath without a struggle.

I thought about bathing my face in cold water but didn't care enough to move. Mary Ann, Mother and Dad crowded everything else out of my mind. I tried concentrating on the wrinkles setting in the sleeves of my suit—trying to guess how long it had taken, sitting here bawling, for my clothes to crinkle up so.

When the chimes rang through the house I felt a surge of relief. Somebody at the door meant I'd have to move, now—Dad wouldn't pay any attention. He probably wouldn't even notice it through the hate he was feeling. Maybe it was Bill Brown!

The ringing kept on while I made myself stand up, and I wiped damp strands of hair out of my face and eyes as I made my way to the door. I opened it expectantly.

Bill Brown was back. I pulled my gaze away from the bitter face and eyes of pain, and saw the figure beside him. I looked back up at Brown and waited for him to explain the scrawny, scared kid inside the yellow-stained suit.

"They got scattered," he said.

"Oh. They did?" I said, trying to place "they" in connection with this kid and the tough gang of hoodlums we hired Brown to bring in. He went on like I hadn't said a word.

"So I decided to bring one at a time. Donald here was handy–and cooperative–so he's first."

And now I got it. Brown wanted to pawn this kid off as one of the kidnappers!

"You're trying to tell me that's a member of the gang?"

"I was lucky, Miss Haas. If you'll let us in you can see what's in the bag I took away from that." He held up a large leather grip and pushed the boy toward the door with his other hand.

They came in and I slammed the door and led the way to the library. Then I announced our arrival to Dad, still buried in his big chair by the window.

"Mr. Brown's back, Dad." He turned and watched.

"Sit over there, Donald," Brown said. He motioned with his hand and the kid sidled over to the chair in an arc that took him furthest out of Brown's reach. The chair was beside Dad's big desk and he propped himself on the front edge, twisting nervously. He watched as Brown unzipped the bag, and tears were brimming in his eyes.

Upside down over the desk, the bag rained packages of bills in a spreading pile before us. Dad jerked his eyes away from the boy, glanced at the money, and looked bleakly at Brown.

"Is that all of it?" he asked.

Brown's head made a slow half-shake, as if he had a stiff neck.

"Part. His part." He pointed at Donald with his thumb; then he reached to the edge of the pile and took out a neat bundle of twenty-dollar bills. "And this is my part of his part. The bonus."

Fees weren't in Dad's mind as his eyes bored holes across the room at the squirming boy on the chair. His knuckles gleamed white around the whipstock hanging down beside his chair, and my eyes traced the snaky length of the lash trailing into the corner behind him. A tingling sensation trickled down my spine and I couldn't decide if it was pleasure or dread. Then Dad started talking.

"So you didn't get away with it, huh, boy?"

"N-no, Sir. Reckon not, Mister."

The admission surprised me. I had expected him to blurt out a denial.

"Why did you kill my little girl, son?" His voice was soft, gentle.

The boy licked his lips, looked at Dad, dropped his eyes again, and was a picture of guilt. I would enjoy what I knew was coming, now—no matter what my dreams would be later. The kid started lying then, too late.

"I didn't hurt her, Mister, honest I never! Nary hair of her head. It wasn't me what done it!" Words tumbled out of his mouth in fear, and he was crying.

"Why did you do it?"

The same chill dripped from Dad's voice. The tension of his hand caused his arm to move slightly and attracted the boy's eyes to the whip for the first time. He fell cringing back against the chair and the blood drained from his face. Words came—fast, shrill, in a high pitch.

"I liked her, I tellya! I never done nothin' to her! I bought her some ice cream an' was good to her an' she was a-callin' me Uncle—"

I heard the short whistling sound which ended with a cruel, wet snap, and a horrible scream broke from his throat and rang through the room. Dad's movement had been a blur. But I was watching Donald and couldn't help seeing the blood spurting from the two halves of his upper lip. It quickly covered his lower face and chin. The lip was split up into one side of his nose and laid back bright and ugly on both sides from the deep gash. His screams came over and over, and his hands were red and slimy from trying to press back the oozing blood. I made myself think of Mary Ann and didn't get sick.

"God!"

That came in a half-gasp, half-gagging noise from Brown standing beside me. A lot of the tan had left his cheeks. He stared, his eyes filmed over like he couldn't believe what he saw—first at Dad, then at the boy. With Donald's weird screams echoing through the library and Brown staring wild and popeyed, the whole scene was from a gruesome nightmare.

Donald finally choked off his screams and started trying to plead with Dad. His eyes, streaming big tears, begged for mercy. His tongue tried to push words through his sobs without the help of his lip, and crimson bubbles built up and burst like atomizer spray.

Crack! Dad's whip crashed through the air again—and this time I did feel just a little sick.

The whip went into the flesh under the kid's left eye and tore a gaping, mushy hole. The boy's eyeball was torn out and hanging by strands of skin, laying on his cheekbone with blood washing over it. Donald half-stood with an animal-like scream, then fell back on his chair in a dead faint.

Brown started yelling.

"Goddamnit, Haas!" He started for Dad. "Give me that whip—there'll be no more—"

"Brown! Get out! Now."

Their eyes locked in a duel, and I knew Brown wanted to take the chance on getting the whip away from Dad. But he turned and walked from the room. I followed right behind and shut the door. He was leaning against the wall with his hand pressed so tight against his forehead the veins protruded, and perspiration glistened on his face.

He looked at me and opened his mouth to say something, but clamped his lips back together and turned away in disgust.

"What did you expect?" I asked.

He whirled.

"Miss Haas. I've been around. I'm a cop—or ex-cop. I've watched, and even helped, the toughest policemen in the world take confessions. When I was sure we were right. But in there I got plain sick."

"I know, Bill," I told him.

"You know nothing! That boy'll very likely be killed in there."

"I wouldn't doubt it."

"Your father will hang if he is. Don't you understand that?"

"I do doubt that. This is Texas you're in."

"I'll be damned if I can stay here and watch while a kid is whipped to death!"

He started for the front door.

"I'll go with you."

"No. I'm going after Junior."

"Don't argue, Bill. Wait out in front. I'll bring a car around."

He went through the door. My car keys were in my purse in the library. Getting a grip on my nerves I opened the door, walked over and picked up the purse and turned to leave.

"Kay."

"I'm leaving for a while, Dad. To help Bi—Mr. Brown."

"Good luck, Kay—but be careful."

"Sure, Dad, I'll be okay."

I hurried out of the room and to the back door. I crossed the garden to the garage and unlocked the Cad convertible, put the top down, and drove around to the front. He had waited but he wasn't happy.

"I'll drive," he said.

"I'll drive," I said.

"Okay, okay, okay!" He got in and almost pulled the door through the side after him. The guy was sore. I was thinking it might be a little stormy after we were married. He was used to having his own way, too. A sweet combination.

"Right now," he said, "Donald's pals are probably waiting for me. Somewhere around the summer amphitheatre at the fairgrounds. My little problem is to persuade one or both to join me."

I reached over and laid my hand on his husky forearm.

"I'll help you, Bill," I promised. He jerked his arm out of reach.

"Thanks." He didn't expect much help from me. "They won't expect me to arrive in such luxury. Maybe I can surprise 'em and get this .45 leveled on one—preferably Junior—and march him into the car. If so, you drive back here while I control his emotions. He's dangerous, but it's just stupid enough to work, driving up and saying hello that way."

"It sounds simple."

"It is. So am I. Or I'd get out of this whole dirty mess. If anything goes wrong and Junior sees Donald like I saw him—it's not too late for you to get out and stay home, with all the doors locked."

"No. I'm going with you, Bill."

"Well, hell—don't just sit there. You're driving, remember? Move it out!"

I did, but too fast, and Bill's head snapped back against the seat. He groaned and grabbed his head in both hands.

"Dear God! Deliver me from Dallas—and women drivers!"

I had to laugh. He turned bleary eyes on me, pawing at his temples.

"There's a box of aspirin in the glove compartment, Bill."

Chapter Fifteen

JUNIOR KNOWLES

When I was shore Donald knowed jes' what to do, I moseyed back down to the big opera buildin' an' walked into them trees at the side. All I had to do was wait for that greedy feller to come an' poke his nose inta my bizness for the last time. I figgered to turn his damper down for good. He musta had a awful hard head to wake up 'thout no help after the black-jackin' I give him before. I'd be shore this time.

'Course, he hadn't never made nothin' offa me, nohow. But he was shore hell on El. An' as long as him an' El was both around he was li'ble to gum up my doin's most any time. I laughed, thinkin' how dumb he was to let El bring him out here to see me; even iff'n he was kinda smart some other ways.

Come to think of it, bringin' him to the fairgrounds was the first thing El hisself had done right since we come to Texas. Iff'n I was able to find out what the man done with El's money I never knowed whether I'd give El any of it back or not. He shore wasn't due nothin', givin' it away like he done. In a little while I heard a flap-flappin'. Sorta like loose corners of a tarp over a load o'cotton, a-blowin' in the wind. When the noise came clos'ter I knowed it was somebody a-runnin', hell-bent for 'lection. I got in the black shadder behind a big tree an' taken out my blackjack. Jes' in case it was Mister Nosey payin' me a call I wanted him to git the right sorta welcomin'.

Purty soon I seen who it was. Ol' El, with his tongue a-hangin' out an' his big feet makin' clompin' noises you coulda heard plumb acrost them fairgrounds, nearly. He come tearin' inta them trees lickety-high-cut an' started yellin' my name out ever' time he could git it outta his fat mouth.

The fool! I shoulda let him bust his brains out ag'in a limb, but I never knowed yet what got him so rambunctious. An' I had to know that. So when he come close to the tree where I was standin' I slung out my foot an' tripped him up. He hit the ground head-first an' come up a-dangin' ever'thing in sight. While he was settin' there I lammed him one in the fat of his rump with my foot.

"Quit yore squawkin', El." He got quiet in a hurry, 'cept for pantin' and' gaspin' for air.

Jes' one good look at his face an' I knowed him an' Donald had got me in some more trouble. As iff'n I never had plenty awready to drive a smart man crazy. Him an' Donald kept a-makin' my load bigger an' bigger. But Donald was my brother—El he wasn't no kin to me. I taken a-holt of his ear an' twisted him up to his feet, him a-squawkin' like a stubborn ol' settin' hen pushed offa her nest.

"Shet up—'fore I give you somethin' to holler about. Where's that there feller was with you? What happened up yonder?"

"Dangit, boy, gimmie a chance't! That there man done took Don's bag o' money away from him!"

I watched him rubbin' his ear, wipin' his neck.

So my brother Donald finally jumped to give away the part of the reward that was his'n. God knowed he'd been a-tryin' to, ever since we split up the money. Jes' like El. Maybe it was catchin'. El's underwear ripped when I grabbed a handful o' hair on his chest an' shaken him back an' forth.

"You derned ol' fool! Tell me what's goin' on!" I was boilin' mad, an' scairt I'd bash his head in 'fore he could tell me.

"Now, wait a minnit, now, Junior, dangit. Awright! I'm a-tellin' fast as I can. . . . Ever'thing was goin' fine. We was on the way down here to find you an' first thing we knowed that feller jerked Don's bag outta his hand! He was a-runnin' when he done it an' got a big head start. He run right inta that place up yonder with the lights in front–an' he's in there now!"

"Keep a-talkin', El. Where's my brother while all this's goin' on?"

"He bought a ticket too an' follered him, yellin' at me to come an' git you. He'll prob'ly stick to that feller like a tick on a jackrabbit 'til you git there, Junior."

"It shore taken you long enough to say so! Le's git up there–quick!"

I was done a-runnin', an' looked back an' seen El tryin' to keep up with me. Maybe I wouldn't be too late, but things was shore gittin' mixed up an' needed some fast fixin'. I begin thinkin' maybe that big stranger was smarter'n I'd give him credit for bein'. Leastways he never done things I figgered him to do.

But smart or dumb up to right now never made no differ'nce a-tall, 'cause I knowed one thing. Jes' let me catch up to him, jes' once't, an' he'd never be smart no more. I was gonna kill him. An' I meant to catch up to him right about now. I slid to a stop in fronta the place an' had me a look around, tryin' to figger the best way of gittin' to Donald an' him. Wasn't nobody around an' the ticket window wasn't open. Reckon they laid off sellin' tickets after Donald got his'n. El come up while I was changin' my bag to the other hand for a rest.

He was all petered out but he was pointin' up the steps to tell me that's how they went in–as iff'n I never figgered that out first thing.

"I'm a-goin' in, El. You stay right here with yore eyes peeled, to make shore they don't come out afore I git back. An' by God you better not miss nothin'!"

Inside it was darker'n pitch 'cept up on a stage in front where some kinda shindig was a-goin' on, with spotlights on the people in the show. There wasn't no moon to speak of an' the light down front 'most blinded me when I tried to see anything out where the people was settin'. They all looked alike. Jes' dim heads an' shoulders, none of 'em movin' a hair an' all of 'em watchin' the stage like blinded cottontails lookin' inta bright headlights.

I done the best I could, but I seen it wasn't no use a-walkin' up an' down beside them rows lookin'. Like tryin' to find a slug o' drinkin' whiskey in a bottle of Coca-Cola. So I left an' went back to where El was a-waitin' on me. He got excited, like always, an' c'menced a-talkin' right off the bat.

"Didja see 'em, Junior? Ya found 'em, didn'tcha?"

"I never looked for 'em."

"But, Junior—"

"Shet yore mouth, old man. Wasn't for yore thinkin' an' talkin' I'd be plumb shut of all this mess now," I told him. "Stand here an' wait some more."

I walked around the place both ways from the steps an' had me a look. Only found two ways to git out besides the front steps. There was another door a little ways back on both sides that I figgered they might open up when the show was over. That made me feel better, only three doors to watch. I knowed I could see ever'body comin' out the front an' same time watch the door on the left side, if need be. Iff'n El couldn't take care of that other side he was a bigger dam' fool than I thought, even.

"El. C'mere!"

"Whatcha found, Junior?"

109

"A hole, fool. You're gonna play like a dam' big tomcat an' watch the hole. From right here."

El was flabbergasted, him not catchin' onta nothin' very easy. But I made it clear to him. I pointed to the door in the side of the buildin'.

"See that there door, El? Iff'n Donald or the other man comes out, or both of 'em t'gether, you gotta light a shuck around to that big tree at the side of the steps an' git me. That's all. You understand?"

"Yeah, Junior. . . . Yeah, I see what I gotta do. But. . . ."

"Shet up, an' start yore watchin'. Ol' man, iff'n they git past you, don't never let me catch up to you."

I went back to my spot an' stood, jes' watchin' an' waitin' an' thinkin'. Time drug by slow as cold molasses. Jes' strainin' my eyes, back an' forth, front an' side, an' back ag'in. I wondered about what time it'd be when the show let out, but it wouldn't a-done me no good—I never had no watch. I lean't back ag'in the tree, an' shifted around ever' so often to rest my back. I was shore tuckered out.

I was gittin' madder an' madder as time went on. It wasn't smart, I knowed, but for two cents I'da run up them steps with my gun an' made somebody put on some lights so's I could find my brother. My teeth was grindin' t'gether like a hound-dog a-worryin' a bone.

When all the clappin' an' whistlin' started inside the buildin' I taken a big breath. I reckoned the show was over an' now we'd git some action an' see who was smart.

I reely had to watch close't. Two outta three chances they'd come out one o' my doors. People come a-rollin' outta them two doors like ants desertin' a hole in the ground, but I managed to git a look at ever' dern one.

Wasn't long 'fore the lines was thinnin' out, an' I never seen hide nor hair of Donald or the feller with his bag of money. I

110

figgered El to come hightailin' it for me any time. But he never come, neither.

Then nobody else was comin' out a-tall, an' lights started blinkin' out like the place was empty. An' I was standin' under the tree by myself, jes' lookin' at nothin' an' tryin' to figger what coulda went wrong.

Then I heard El clompin' up an' I swung around, hopin'!

"Whichaway did they go, El?"

"Didn't you see 'em neither, Junior? They never come out my . . . Junior! They never come out on my side, now, an' I'm shore o' that! Don'tcha try to say they. . . . Reely, Junior—you seen 'em, didn't you?"

"Iff'n I seen 'em would I be standin' here a-listenin' to yore blabber? I'm goin' in for another look."

Inside I got a good look all around. The place was flat empty, 'cept for coke bottles, paper cups, popcorn sacks an' such scattered from hell to breakfast all over. I went back outside.

"They give us the slip, El. You better be a-hopin' when I find my brother he don't say they come out yore door."

"Aw, Junior—Don wouldn't wanta give you the slip, would he?"

"Naw."

"What we gonna do, Junior?"

"I ain't got the slightes' idy, El."

El blinked at me an' his mouth fell open. First thing he ever ast me I couldn't answer, I reckon. But I'd spoke the truth. I never had no idy a-tall, 'ceptin' this Dallas was a awful big place with Donald somewhere in it.

I never even knowed which way he went.

"Y'ain't gonna let the stranger keep our money, are ya? Huh, Junior, y'aint, are ya?"

111

Jes' lookin' at him an' listenin' made me sicker to my stummick than wonderin' about Donald. I made up my mind, once't an' for all.

"El, goddamnit, you git away from me—you hear? I don't never wanta see you ag'in! Git, now!"

"But Junior . . . what's got inta you? We're friends, ain't we? You're joshin' me, ain'tcha?"

"Ol' man, do like I'm a-tellin, you—while you can."

"I swear, Junior, I cain't figger you out, son. Where ya want me to go?"

"El, I'm astin' you to save yore fool life. Best way to do it is git away from me."

"Dangit, Junior, I cain't go nowheres a-tall 'thout no money. I ain't even got a car no more since you taken it—an' 'at's all I ever did have, that car. You know it, boy!"

I watched him. Looked as if he was gonna bust out cryin' most any time. I helt m'self off'n him an' unzipped my bag, an' taken out a stack of fives an' throwed it at him. He caught it one-handed.

"Git!" I told him, ag'in.

He was blubberin' an' snifflin' when he walked off, a-scuffin' his shoes on the pavement. But he never knowed how lucky he was. Iff'n I ever seen him ag'in he was a dead duck, 'cause I jes' couldn't stummick him no more. He'd brung me nothin' but trouble, this here whole mess o' trouble.

I felt lower'n a snake's belly in a wagonrut. I sat down ag'in the tree, wonderin' what to do now. El wasn't in sight no more an' all the lights was out around the doors. It was still as a graveyard. I was dog-tired, as who wouldn't a-been, an' I musta dozed a little bit settin' there.

Then there was a gunbarrel stickin' in my neck. Funny how I knowed what it was when I couldn't see it. That's somethin' you jes' know 'thout bein' told, I reckon–but I was told, besides.

"It's a gun, Junior," somebody behind me said. "Now if I were you and had all that cash, I'd have a room in one of the better hotels–the Baker, say. All right, ON YOUR FEET!"

I shore called *myself* some bad names while I got up. Me, Junior Knowles, gittin' trapped sleepin', right at the sidewalk! I never looked around to see who was holdin' the gun. I had a dern good idy, 'thout lookin'. I wondered how he knowed me, an' guessed my bag had give me away, it bein' jes' like Donald's which he had took.

"Just take two steps forward. Hold it, now."

He patted me up an' down an' jerked my blackjack outta my hip pocket. Then he taken my gun an' the roll of exter bills I'd been a-usin' to pay for little things that come up. He clucked his tongue like at a kid.

"Concealed weapons! The law wouldn't like that, Junior."

I never said nothin' but I was thinkin' plenty.

"Now walk, easy, toward the street. And make one move I don't like. It'll be your last. I'll bring your bag–you look tired."

I done like he said an' walked slow an' easy. He shore had a mean voice. The gun wasn't touchin' me no more but my back wrinkled up while he talked jes' the same. He hated me, an' now he had all the reward money, an' I 'spected a bullet to bang inta me any time. He had the whole fifteen thousand dollars! I hated myself bad as he did, for not killin' him the first time I laid eyes on him. I got nearly to the street.

"Hold it, Junior," he said.

I stood right still an' a big car come a-floatin' down the street an' up to the curb. It was a Caddalac, bran'-spankin' new, with the top down, an' drivin' it was one o' the purtiest gals I ever seen.

"All right, Junior. Get in–easy."

113

I was thinkin' about how a man couldn't live forever, nohow, an' it shore looked like my time to kick the bucket had done come. I never had nothin' to lose, an' was gittin' outsmarted ever' time I turned around—which hurt me bad. That there voice sounded close't behind me, so I made up my mind quick to win, lose or draw.

I opened the door o' the car an' kicked, straight back behind me, jes' like a mule. My foot landed jes' where I hoped for. The gun clattered an' slid acrost the sidewalk an' offa the curb an' my money bag thumped to the ground. I turned around slick as a whistle an' swung my fist at the stranger's chin. Like shootin' fish in a barrel, 'cause he was busy holdin' where he was hurtin' with both hands an' groanin'. He went down like a poleaxed steer in a slaughter chute.

Still movin' fast as lightnin' I dove for the gun an' come up, a-stickin' the end of it in the gal's face. I grabbed the purse she was fumblin' with an' throwed it outta her reach. She jes' couldn't figger out what was happenin'. Reckon I was too quick for her. An' now I was boss ag'in.

"Set there, gal. An' jes' set there!"

I kept a eagle eye on her while I got my bag an' I throwed it in the car. Then I drug the big smart feller, who wasn't smart enough to tangle horns with me, over to the curb, rollin' an' pushin' an' liftin' him, tryin' to git him inside on the floorboards. He groaned once't, but he was helpless as a ol' cow in labor, an' dam' nigh as heavy. Stuffin' him in there was like manhandlin' a bale o' cotton into a wagonbed by myself but I done it. I taken my blackjack an' gun an' roll of bills offa him—outta the side pockets of a fancy suit he was a-wearin', then I got in.

"Where's Donald at, gal?"

She jes' lifted them narrer black eyebrows and said, "Donald? Who's he?"

114

Jes' to keep the talk 'twixt us two I whomped down on nosey's head with the gunbarrel. Figgered maybe that'd have more 'fect on him than my blackjack had the last time. He quit groanin' an' got real quiet, an' the gal taken the hint. She done better next time we talked.

"Where's my brother at?"

"He's at my house."

"That's better—git to drivin'! I got a hankerin' to see him."

She started the big car an' rolled it down the street tords the gate. I tapped her on the shoulder with the gun an' she cut her eyes at me.

"One peep, gal, jes' one, will git you a bullet right in yore stummick."

She was so scairt she jes' nodded an' rolled out the gate an' started through town.

It never taken long to git there.

We rolled up in fronta the house with them big porch poles. Now I knowed the answer. Mr. Haas had my brother Donald! Mighta killed him for all I knowed. Most likely was gonna turn him over to the law, though.

"Mr. Haas yore dad, gal?"

She nodded 'thout lookin' at me. She musta liked the bum on the floorboards, way she looked at him kinda pitiful-like.

"Anybody here, 'sides him an' my brother?"

She shaken her head no.

"Git out."

She did, while I cracked her friend over the head ag'in nearly hard enough to break the gunbarrel—so's to make shore he'd stay put a while this time. His head was bleedin' right good. I was gonna kill him in some special way I never had figgered out yet. I wanted him a-waitin' when I come out with Donald.

I made the gal go up to the front door an' motioned her to open it up. Her hand was shakin' so much she couldn't git

the key in an' I had to take it away from her an' do it myself.
I opened the door an' shoved her in front o' me, an' stuck her
keys in my pocket. We went down a hall, an' her knees musta
been weak, way she went from side to side an' helt herself
away from the walls. Scairt, I reckon. She come to a door an'
opened it, so I pushed her in an' stuck my head in after.

What I seen give me a awful jolt. Donald was layin' on the
floor in the middle of a big puddle of blood. Hard to tell it
was him, he was so cut up. He never had no eyes an' his
whole face put me in mind of a rag soaked in blood an' piled
up on itself. Mr. Haas looked up from a chair acrost the room
an' seen me.

He had him a long whip an' I seen his arm start to draw it
back for a cut at me, so I squeezed the trigger. A hole come in
his face jes' between the nose an' mouth. The hole musta
went all the way through, 'cause loose brains started runnin'
down the chair where they was spillin' out the back o' his
head. The gal screamed an' I made a swipe at her with my
gun. It caught her 'longside the head an' she fell on the floor.
I shoulda emptied the gun inta her, an' reckon I would've
iff'n I hadn't a-been so worried about my brother.

I seen he was still alive. I hadta get Donald outta there, to a
doctor!

Fast!

I grabbed a fancy Mex shawl offa one o' the tables an' rolled
Donald into it as gentle as I could. He soaked right through
it, but I carried him out an' went for the big Caddalac. That's
when I shore saw red an' swore a blue-curdlin' streak. That
big feller was gone! Ag'in!

I shore wanted to look for that man. He couldn't a-got far.
But I never had no time for that now.

I hadta git my brother to a doctor, first off. He was so still I
was scairt he mighta died since I brung him outta the house.

116

I felt the big blood vessel in his neck an' his heart was still a-pumpin'. Slow, but it was pumpin' some.

I fished the gal's keys outta my pocket an' jumped in the car. I set still a minute to try to quit shakin'. I never been so upset in all my born' days. Finally it got some better an' I started the engine.

I shoved the big car in gear an' reckon I burn't rubber in the gravel o' that driveway when I gunned it outta there, but I was in high when I hit the street.

CHAPTER SIXTEEN

FRED CAMPBELL

This entire case was nothing less than a studied insult to Dallas.

What's more, and I took it as a personal affront, the insults kept right on piling up. One on top of the other. I knew if the stack got much higher it was likely to crumble from its own weight—with one Lieutenant Fred Campbell of Homicide marooned in the middle of the debacle.

I wondered if anyone knew that I was in charge of this case? Any of the principals, I mean. I was well aware that some several of my superior officials knew I was—and that they were unreasonably impatient for results.

And *I* knew I was in charge, all right—and kept regretting the fact.

At this time of the year I should be out shooting doves. Or even skeet. Fishing. Or something. Instead of wishing I'd chosen a more practical vocation.

Damnedest case we ever had. My hunch was that this business was the work of well-trained thugs from the East, but there was nothing tangible for the tie-up. I didn't know much, and was sure of nothing. In fact, everyone else and his brother seemed to know more about what had already happened and what was going on now than I did. What a life.

Here I sat. Cooling my heels in the living room of the late Mr. Galin Haas–who was shot through the face by someone. What was it the Haas girl had said?

"Junior shot my father, Lieutenant. On account of his brother. But there isn't time to tell you all about it right now– Mr. Brown was badly hurt and I must look after him."

And with that she had hurried off up the stairs. What a woman! What filled my eyes also crowded argument out of my mind. No man could watch Miss Haas hurry up a flight of stairs from down below and keep his thoughts on the legitimate business at hand. But now that she was out of sight I made myself go over it again.

Junior . . . there must be thousands of Juniors in Dallas, but I couldn't recall any of the local bad boys with that name or alias. And 'on account of his brother' wasn't too informative. Whose brother? Junior's brother? Miss Haas' father's brother? My brother, maybe. Maybe I was going nuts. . . . 'Mister Brown'. . . .

Mister, phooey. Bill Brown. Fugitive from a hotel room loaded with ransom money. I wanted to talk to him–bad. I said so the next time Miss Haas made the quick trip down and up with items to comfort the injured crook.

"No," she had said. "He really doesn't feel up to talking about anything now. The pain ruined his sleep last night. He's napping a bit now, and you'll just have to wait."

This little act was giving me a pain that would keep me awake, too, but I didn't tell her so. I was waiting. And while I did my brain was going through the dog-chases-tail routine.

Anyone could see the kidnapping had been planned to perfection. Probably one of the reference texts had been Dun & Bradstreet. There are a lot of well-known, well-to-do men in Dallas and a lot of them have daughters. But Galin Haas, while he was the rich man of Dallas, had kept it nicely to himself and few outsiders knew it. Too, of all the others I could think of, none of them had daughters as young as Mary Ann. And she had been an ideal age for kidnapping. It was a devilishly clever operation all the way down the line.

The Negro girl had been paid off by the mob, probably– we'd find out about that when we found her. The little girl gone, the money paid as ordered without a protest; and then after it was all over the Haas clan had condescended to call on the department for a little help. Mighty white of them–to dump all their negative information in my lap. Damned decent.

Mary Ann Haas–dead. Galin Haas–dead. The killers–gone. One suspect available–now resting comfortably–napping, that is–in Galin Haas' bed. And he doesn't wish to be disturbed! By God!

The goat? The Homicide Bureau, meaning, literally, Fred Campbell.

Well, we'd see about that!

Miss Haas came down the stairs again and broke up my soliloquy.

"Mr. Brown will speak to you now, Lieutenant."

"Well! Will he, now? That's really nice of him. Shall I knock, or just go right in?" You'd have thought this Bill Brown was a hundred-grand-a-year executive granting five minutes to a handmade tie salesman, instead of rating the Number One entry on my list.

"I'll go in with you, Lieutenant," Miss Haas said.

"That won't be necessary, Miss Haas. Our conversation may. . . ."

"Just follow me, Lieutenant. And please be brief—the nurse wants to give him some broth shortly."

"Why, I wouldn't want him to miss out on *that*. Lead on, Miss Haas."

I followed her up the stairs, wondering how any woman could appear so cold mentally and emotionally, yet make me feel so uncomfortably warm, interested and guilty in her presence. I went into the room behind her and found I was almost tiptoeing in spite of my loathing for this Brown who basked in her protective custody.

I didn't like his looks. Prejudice, maybe. Maybe even jealousy, too. But that's the way I felt. His head was wrapped in bandages but he wore an insolent grin on his pan. As to the grin, I somehow got the feeling it was mostly forced—that he wasn't as carefree a tramp as he looked. But he was stretched out in the large canopied bed as if he owned it and had never slept in a boxcar in his life.

All in all, and still admitting possible jealousy, he was a typical, no-good bum if I ever saw one.

"Miss Haas said you'd like to talk to me, Lieutenant."

"She was right. Brown, I am, so to speak, interested in this kidnapping, extortion, and the murders. Considering my position, I'm sure you'll agree that's normal. I'm particularly interested to know just how you fit into these things."

"Sure, Lieutenant—I fit like this: In the employ of Miss Haas. They, she and her father, hired me. To find some kidnappers for them."

"I see—but not too clearly yet. It so happens that I'm employed by the citizenry of Dallas—to find the kidnappers for them."

"Meaning I'll have help? Or should I say competition?"

"Meaning neither, Brown. Meaning that right now, and with no malicious intent to shock a sick man, understand, I am seriously toying with the idea of labeling you a kidnapper. Which would, of course, end with you locked up in jail."

"A mistaken idea, Lieutenant. I'm no kidnapper."

"I've got enough evidence to see you convicted, mistake or not. Has that occurred to you?"

"I'll admit I gave it some thought. But it won't hold."

"A mere difference of opinion."

"No—more than that. Too many loose ends. You couldn't cover them all up, Lieutenant."

"When you know me better, Brown, you'll know I gave it a hell of a good try."

"You want to know something, Lieutenant? I've changed my mind about you, somewhat. It'll cost me, but I think I'll tell you what I know."

"It's good of you to offer—I was wondering if I'd have to forget my manners and come right out and ask you, point-blank."

He told me. A highly absorbing yarn that didn't touch my personal theory at any point. The trouble was it was just impossible and screwy enough that it could have some, or none, or a hell of a lot of truth in it. A pay-your-money-and-take-your-choice kind of narrative. I thought personally the licks on Brown's head had stimulated his imagination. I didn't expect it to pan out and I knew he was holding out on me. But at least I had something to go on—to see if any of it could be verified. I took up the phone off the bedside stand and put a call through to the man covering the bus station.

"Al, check the station for a fat and slouchy individual as follows: Sore, red nose, appearance of an Okie clodbuster, wearing a dirty undershirt under his coat and minus any socks. Call me back here." I read him the number off the plate on the phone base, hung up, rolled a cigarette, and waited.

The nurse came in with a bowl of chicken broth, the smell of which reminded me that I wasn't eating with my usual regularity. She started feeding it to Brown and the slob winked at me between spoonfuls. He was getting real service and he knew it. But it was to get even better.

Miss Haas came in and took over.

"I'll feed him, nurse," she said.

"Yes, Ma'am." The nurse's reluctance was disgustingly obvious as she surrendered her duties to Miss Haas and left the room. All of which only served to irritate me more and more. What the hell they saw in him I don't know. The phone rang and I jumped to answer it. It was Al. I listened to his report. A strike!

"Okay, Al. Find out if his name is Mercer—Elsworth Mercer."

It was. "Hold him. Take him in and book him for investigation in the kidnapping. Don't let anyone get to him before I can see him . . . Right. I'll be down later . . . What the hell is that, Al? Al! Hello! Hello! What the. . . ."

It sounded like Al had thrown the phone against the wall and I could hear a commotion coming over the wire, shouting that faded away after a moment, then nothing except a faint rustle of sounds like you might expect to hear around a bus station. Then came what sounded like a shot. The guy must have made a break for it! I breathed a prayer that Al wouldn't throw a .38 slug into some bystander, and was so impatient I felt like gnawing on the receiver. I kept it glued to my ear and tried to catch a mental picture of the action but all I caught was a faint echo of a woman's scream following the shot.

I grabbed the directory and got the number of the ticket office, broke my connection and dialed it–and got a busy signal; twice; three times. I hung up, thinking if Al didn't call me back his family was going to get hungry.

"Cops! I guess El heard you guys talking about him and your friend Al just let him walk away," Brown said. I resented the sarcasm but I had no way of knowing how near right he was.

"Something happened–I don't know what, yet. But Al will call me as soon as he can. By the way, if Mercer gets clear where are you supposed to meet him?"

"Now, Lieutenant, that's unreasonable–didn't I put him on the spot for you?"

It was true. No sense in antagonizing him when he'd given me the first lead I'd had that amounted to a hill of beans.

"Sorry. But just remember you're not in the clear, Brown, simply by throwing someone else to the lions."

"Forget it. And don't worry–I'm clean."

I grunted. Why didn't Al call back? I had to use that phone, just in case some more of Brown's story was the McCoy. I risked missing out with Al and called the office. Nothing there as to Al. There was a lot to do, but I made it as brief as I could and still keep it accurate.

The description of the Cad to get out to the road blocks; the description of Junior, with a caution about his quick trigger-finger; instructions for a recheck on all motels, hotels and rooming houses; on doctors, quacks, chiropractors–hell, practically everyone in the city, as the clerk on the phone insinuated before I was through.

That's what makes police work thankless, this all-embracing check and eliminate, check and eliminate, of anything and everything a criminal might think of. Good police work anticipates his thoughts, but in this case the trail was already a good eight hours cold. Not good, because a man on the run will think of a great many angles in eight hours. We'd have trouble gaining on him. I must have been getting jumpy–I was startled when the phone rang. It was Al.

"Hello. Yes, Campbell here . . . What? . . . Oh, hell! . . . Well, don't feel too bad–these things happen, that's all. . . . Anybody else hurt? Well, that's one consolation. Look, Al– I don't think anything will come of this down your way, but. . . ."

I gave him Junior's description and told him to keep an eye out for him, just in case. Then I turned to Brown.

"One in your favor. Mercer won't be testifying against you. He made a break, ran out on the ramp. Al fired in the air to stop him, but when Mercer looked around he didn't stop running. He was crushed between a bus rolling into the station and another one standing idle on the ramp. Spread him like a pancake. The driver felt the impact and pulled away from the standing bus and hit his brakes–just as Mercer fell under the rear duals. They pulled it off of him, but he was dead when the ambulance got there."

"Jesus Christ," was all Brown had to say.

Damnedest case I ever saw. Well, I had to get on with it.

"Miss Haas, I'll be going now, but I'll leave a couple of good men here at the house for your protection."

"I appreciate your offer, Lieutenant, but I shan't need them. Mr. Brown is here."

"That's right, Lieutenant–be glad to keep an eye on her. Both eyes."

"Thanks, Brown, but due to your condition, not to mention other considerations, I'll leave some men just the same."

Miss Haas didn't like it.

"I'll not have policemen, in or out of uniform, in or near my house! That's final. It isn't me you're worried about—you think Mr. Brown is guilty of something. Well, he isn't."

She meant what she said, apparently, so I shrugged. I'd have to hide them out somewhere in the neighborhood.

"All right, Miss Haas. But I don't think it's a wise course. We'll try to get your car back."

"Get me the murderer, Lieutenant."

"Him, too. He can't go far. If these stories I've picked up here will hold water, he'll try for medical attention for his brother. All highways and outlets are covered—have been since the first meager information we got about this case. I believe he's still in Dallas. He won't get out alive if he is."

"He won't go anywhere alive if I see him again," she said.

"Oh, yeah. I meant to speak to you about that. I don't want any more interference from you, Miss Haas—or you either, Brown. Especially you."

"What?" she practically screamed at me. "How can you say that? If it hadn't been for Mr. Brown you'd still be helplessly lost. He's done more than you and your whole police force!"

I counted slowly to twenty-five under my breath before I could answer. Why? Because she was probably the richest living taxpayer in Dallas, and my pay comes from the coffers of the city treasury. The fewer influential taxpayers who register complaints concerning Fred Campbell, the more likely it is to continue coming from that source.

"Yes, ma'am," I was forced to agree. But I threw a dig at Brown. "I have an idea Bill Brown just might be your real name. Mind telling me if it's a phoney?"

"Why would I use a phoney?"

"Do you think it would do me any good to check with Los Angeles on that name?"

125

"Check for what?" He acted surprised. Too surprised.

"We'll see. By the way—consider yourself under arrest."

Miss Haas got huffy again.

"Now why should he be? He's done nothing but help me—and you! Is that the thanks he gets?"

"He's a very material witness," I said, trying to soothe her. "Also, he admitted candidly to outright theft of a suitcase from a locker in the bus station—remember? We can't allow that sort of thing, Miss Haas. Not in Dallas." I was edging toward the door. "Well, I'll keep you informed—and would appreciate your doing the same for me."

"Goodbye, Lieutenant," she said.

"So long, Lieutenant," Brown said. "Hey, you got any spare aspirins on you?"

"You can't have any more yet," his beautiful custodian told him.

I shook my head, meaning more than just no. He was henpecked, but he really had something along with it. I went on downstairs, out the front door, and got into my official car.

"Anything new come over?"

My driver shook his head.

I spat words into the mike. "Fred Campbell will be at the station for the next hour. For the next hour. Over and out."

Bob let the clutch in and started downtown.

This entire case was nothing less than a studied insult to Dallas.

And Dallas paid the salary of Lieutenant Fred Campbell.

CHAPTER SEVENTEEN

Junior Knowles

The tires on that Caddalac whined like a lonesome screech-owl, when I busted outta the driveway an' jerked it to the right an' taken out up the street.

I never knowed which way to go—nor where I'd wind up 'fore it was over. I jes' knowed Donald had to git some doctorin' an' he had to git it P. D. Q. or it wouldn't help him none. I was in such a to-do I was goin' faster'n I calc'lated an' when I seen the speedometer I jerked my foot off'n the gas an' slowed down. This here wasn't no time to have some dumb constabull take after us an' git us both.

Goin' slower I could think better, too—an' it shore was a time to do some. Here on out, ever'thing I done was jes' natcherly gonna be cram-full o' danger. No gittin' around that. First thing, I made up my mind to git Donald in bed in a cabin in some tourist camp. An' I'd git a doctor to come an' take care of him in the cabin. Drivin' that big shiny car an' macked out in my new clo'es, an' with all the money I could flash around, I figgered gittin' inta some high-class tourist camp would be a dead cinch.

By that time I was gittin' out sorta in the edge o' town so I c'menced a-lookin' for a camp that'd suit me. Iff'n that big stranger had come to hisself an' wasn't a-scairt to he mighta called the police. Iff'n he did they could be watchin' for that

Caddalac, so I knowed it wouldn't hurt none to git it outta sight right off.

After drivin' around a little I seen a place that taken my fancy. It was a purty-lookin' spread with the office-buildin' all rimmed in blue neon light a-runnin' ever whichaway. The brick cabins was built around a green yard which had a big fountain in the middle with water shootin' inta the air an' colored lights a-flickerin' all over it. A uppity place, awright. I drove the car inta the openin' 'twixt the trees in front.

Nobody couldn't see Donald nohow, but I went a piece past the office 'fore I stopped, jes' to make shore. I walked back an' banged on the door. A big tall feller with patches o' gray hair opened it. He was in fancy pajameys an' acted like he was mad about somethin'.

"The sign yonder says 'No Vacancy', Mister—didn't you read it?" this feller said.

"Read this here, yoreself," I told him. I shoved a crackly new twenty-dollar bill inta his long bony hand. He could read it, awright. He stuffed it in the pocket of his pajamey coat, an' his idys changed mighty sudden-like.

"Just a minute, sir; I'll get some keys and see what we can do."

Seein' money shore put that feller in high gear—he come up with a big key ring right away, throwed on a bathrobe, an' come out. He taken me down to the third cabin, an' he sorta giggled to hisself when he swung the door open.

"Here you are, sir. Lucky, that's all I can say. I thought maybe this couple'd be gone by now—heh, heh, heh!"

I never liked that there laugh o' his'n an' wished I had time to teach him a lesson on mindin' his own bizness. But I couldn't have no truck with nobody till I got Donald fixed up. I walked inta the cabin with him an' wrote 'Zeb Rice' on the card he told me to sign. Then I kinda s'prised him when he ast if they was anything else he could do for me.

"Yeah, they is somethin' else. You can git me a dang good doctor up here to my cabin–quick. A eye doctor'd be best."

"Eye doctor? This time of night?"

"Eye doctor's what I said. My eyes is hurtin' somethin' awful."

"But I don't know any eye doctors, Mister. Why not wait 'til mornin' and go to one's office?"

He shore was a slow man to deal with. I peeled off another twenty for him to read an' handed it over. Then I thumbed through my roll for a one an' give him that'n too.

"Here, feller–now do like I tellya, willya? Change that dollar inta nickels an' start ringin' up some eye doctors in the phone book. I ain't astin' for nothin' free–an' doctors likes money, same as you. Now hurry up, you hear?"

"Yes, sir! I'll see. I'll sure do my best."

Rate we was goin' he'd prob'ly sew on more pockets an' hope I'd fill 'em up for him. That last twenty got hid in his bathrobe pocket mighty fast, leastways, an' he lit out.

I drove the car inta the lean-to garage, an' I pulled Donald out careful, an' toted him to the bed. I fixed what was left o' him as comfy as I could an' turn't the fan on. Even the nights in Big D was hot. I fetched some wet towels from the toilet an' I laid one over Donald's face so's he wouldn't be bothered by the light an' so's I wouldn't hafta see his face.

He never had come to himself yet an' he was breathin' hard outta his chopped up nose. At least he was alive, an' maybe the doctors could fix up his eyes some. Lookin' at him made me sorry I'd killed ol' man Haas so easy an' quick. I shoulda drug it out an' give him what he give Donald, right back, an' then let him die slow an' painful. I started walkin' the floor

129

wonderin' what that dam' manager was doin' to take so long.
I locked the cabin door an' went to find out.

He was phonin', awright. He musta been waitin' for a answer
when I got there, 'cause he halt the receiver ag'in his ear an'
started talkin' to me.

"Fourth one I've called, Mister. Don't seem like they wanta
come out."

"Who's 'at on the phone now?"

"This's a Doctor Mercedes—or rather, his wife answered
and has gone to get him."

"Gimmie that phone." I taken it an' waited till the doctor
come.

"Doctor! You gotta come an' help me. Quick! I'll pay you
good, an' you gotta come. I'm goin' blind—my eyes feels like
fiery coals an' I cain't see. Don't even know where I'm at.
The manager'll tellya."

I jammed the phone inta the manager's hand an' give him
a hard look. "Give him this here address an' back up what I
said to him."

He done what I said but he give me a awful funny look
when he hung up.

"He won't like us tellin' him lies. Says he don't live far and
will come right over—but he's gonna cost you."

"I can stand it, feller. Never you mind—'cept yore own
bizness. I never give you that there money to mind mine."

I started out to go to the cabin, but I had another idy.

"When he gits here, send him to the cabin—don't bring him.
I don't want nobody hangin' around to see iff'n I holler when
he pokes around in my eyes."

"Don't worry. I'll just be glad to got some sleep, Mister."

"You better git at least forty dollars worth."

Donald wasn't breathin' so hard when I got back. I never
knowed iff'n that was a good sign or not. I soaked a towel in

130

warm water an' started a-washin' some o' the dried blood off'n his neck an' hands, bein' gentle as a cow lickin' her calf. Then I happened to think of somethin' an' I run out to the car.

Here I'd done let that bag o' money lay around in the car all that time I was a-messin' around! I was shore gonna hafta be more careful an' keep my mind on my bizness. Gawda-mighty! Leonie!

Leonie'd be in Dallas in the mornin'! I'd had so dern much a-houndin' me I'd plumb forgot about her. Well, there was some hours yet 'fore she'd pull in, an' I'd hafta cross that there bridge when I come to it. I'd hafta change my idy 'bout me an' Leonie livin' in Dallas now, on account o' me bein' hunted for stealin' a car an' shootin' ol' man Haas besides ever'thing else. People was beginnin' to know me by sight. I was a-hopin' I'd git one more chance't at that feller what started mosta this here trouble—I still couldn't believe no man could have a head so hard he could git around after the way I beat him on it. That there Haas gal, too—she got off with only a bump on her noggin'.

An' jes' lookit what they done to my brother! Now me an' him was jes' like hunted maddogs. Anybody that seen us'd start shootin' on sight, most likely. Soon as Donald could be jostled some we was gonna hafta run for it an' git 'way away from Dallas.

Two things I knowed. I wasn't goin' nowheres 'thout Leonie, an' 'fore we left Donald was to be took care of. I'd manage it all some way—up to now I had an' nobody hadn't hurt me yet, an' I still had my money. Figgered I was about to spend some, too, 'cause a car come in the camp an' stopped at the office an' I could hear that manager a-talkin' to somebody.

I shet off the light an' opened the cabin door jest a crack. The manager was pointin' the cabin out to a feller carryin' a li'l handbag so I felt easier. It must be the doctor finally come to help Donald, I thought.

I switched the light on an' when he got to the door I let him in.

"C'mon in, Doctor."

He grunted an' looked around, blinkin' in the light. He seen my brother an' walked over by the side o' the bed, lookin' down at him. He taken the towel off'n his face an' it fell outta his hand onta the floor.

"Holy Mother of God!" said this here doctor. I never knowed doctors was that squeamish, but this'n was.

Donald wasn't movin', not a quiver. He was still out colder'n a wedge, but in a ugly sort of a way he kinda looked happy to me. Reckon that was 'cause a lot o' his face was missin' an' I could see his teeth plumb to the back of his mouth–put me in mind of a big wide grin.

That doctor wasn't a-grinnin' when he looked at me ag'in, though.

"What in the world has happened to this boy?"

"Tellin' you that wouldn't do him no good, Doctor. I'm awful worried 'bout him. Please hurry up an' fix him while you got time, won'tcha?"

"Fix him! Man, are you crazy? I can't touch him! Phone for an ambulance–he'll have to go to a hospital, immediately."

"Naw, Doc. Fix him here an' now. He's lost too much blood awready to go a-gallivantin' around some more."

"He'll have to. . . . If it's money, there's a County Hos–"

"It ain't money, Doc. It's time. An' you ain't doin' nothin' for him with yore talk."

He bent down an' opened his li'l bag.

"I'll do what I can first, certainly. But what I can do won't be near enough. His condition's critical–you must believe that–get him to a place for proper care."

He started messin' around with Donald's face. Purty soon I was seein' eye to eye with him on what he said about him not doin' near enough. He jes' dabbed an' bandaged an' dabbed some more—looked like he was scairt to do anything. I had to say somethin'.

"Doc. Ain'tcha gonna sew up them rips in his fact afore you put them bandages on?"

"I can't do that work here! It'll take time, equipment, assistants—he must go where they are available."

"You got that sorta stuff in yore office, Doc?"

"My office is in my residence—quite well equipped, but it's no hospital."

"Then le's take him to yore place—that'd be better'n this, I reckon?"

He looked at me, disgusted, an' straightened up from bendin' over Donald.

"You must be a lunatic. But try to understand me. This boy's condition is dangerous. I'm sure you're the man I talked with on the phone. Your whole attitude reeks of secrecy, and I may as well tell you now I'm forced to report this incident to the police."

"Shore, Doc, shore—I'm gonna report it myself. But he needs some help first. Then we'll do the reportin' accordin' to however you say."

"Damn it, man, nothing more can be done until he's in proper hands!"

The Doc had me in a sweat, an' now Donald was fixin' to make things worse. He was comin' to hisself a little, an' started groanin', an' his fingers was a-twitchin' like he was wantin' to reach for help but was too puny. Made me plumb desperate.

"Doc, le's carry him up to yore place. Maybe we can put him to bed on a cot or somethin'. You could give him some shots, whatever you got, an' put him to sleep while you worked on them cuts. Lookit him! He's suffer'n', terrible!"

"Take the boy to a hospital."

This here doctor had ast me iff'n it was money kept me from takin' Donald to a hospital. I sorta wondered iff'n the doctor hisself could maybe use a li'l exter money. After all, he'd clumb out of a good warm bed to come out there an' make a few dollars.

I poked around in the bag an' hauled out a stack of tens. I eyed Doc an' riffled the ends o' them bills like a deck o' poker cards. They was new, o' course, an' made a nice noise.

"Doc. Wouldja help us for money?"

He looked at them tens like he was countin' 'em in his head. But his head was shakin' side to side.

"No. There's something wrong about all this. I won't be a party to it, except my report to the police."

I roughed the edges o' them tens ag'in. I'd awready learn't to let money do mosta my argyin'. His eyes come back to 'em.

"Listen here, Doc. They's two hunderd an' fifty dollars in this here li'l stack. For a hour's work or so."

"No."

"Wait, Doc—I ain't through. This here's whatcha git now—jes' like a deposit on a piece o' land. When I leave yore place with Don—with my friend, you git the rest o' yore pay. It'll be another stack jes' like this'n."

He was a-weakenin'! I seen it in his face.

"An' nobody'll never know, Doc. We can git outta there 'fore daylight an' you can be shore I won't tell nobody nothin'." I give a li'l laugh to convince him whatever was a-keepin' me away from hospitals would keep my trap shet about him.

I tossed the money at him an' he caught it 'most as neat as ol' El done when I run him off. I knowed I'd git it back from Doc 'fore I left. I coulda promised him plenty more but I never wanted to overdo it an' ruin the trap.

I reckon even some doctors owes poker debts or past-due bills of some kind. Anyhow he never throwed it back at me.

He said, "We'll go in my car," an' headed for the door.

I got my hand on the gun under my coat an' follered him. He was my only chance't, an' iff'n he tried to git away they'd have him to bury. But he jes' started his car an' backed it up to the cabin door. We put Donald in easy as we could, then clumb in ourselfs. When we was all set the Doc drove off.

Later on I was satisfied the Doc was tryin' to earn his pay. We had my brother laid out on a operatin' table in the Doc's office an' he was workin' real hard over him. His ol' lady had come in to help. She musta helped him lots o' times–she knowed what she was a-doin'. The painkiller Doe shot inta Donald done the trick, too, an' he was a-restin' purty easy when they got done, seemed to me like.

"How 'bout his eyes, Doc–any chance't?"

"That's hard to say so soon but I don't think he'll ever see. A very slight chance for the right one, but I doubt it. I'll tell you once more–get him to a hospital."

"Now, Doc, we done settled all that."

"It's up to you, if you want him to die of shock. I've done all I can for now and I'd better call and report this case. What happened–you've never said."

"That's right, Doc. I ain't never said."

He started for the phone but I slipped my gun outta my belt. I'd done picked out a place for him an' his ol' lady.

"Jes' hold it, Doc; you an' yore wife stand right over here t'gether facin' the wall."

They couldn't argy, an' done like I said. I taken my money outta Doc's pocket.

"Thanks, Doc. Now, both o' you git inta that there little closet."

Once't they was inside I locked 'em in an' hollered through the door at 'em.

"Now, iff'n y'all are quiet I won' t hafta shove no rags in yore mouth. One holler or yap an' you both git stuffed." Wasn't no answer from inside.

I was about caught up on my figgerin' now. I was dog-tired an' flopped down in a soft chair. This was gonna be a long night, but we'd be safeter here than anywhere's else till mornin'. Me an' Donald we could both use some rest, an' I was purty shore they wouldn't find the Caddalac 'fore the next day sometime. By then I hoped to git Leonie at the bus station, an' would know more 'bout whether I could risk takin' Donald with me when I seen how he made the night.

I knowed I couldn't set up all night. I went an' locked the front door an' then the back, an' pulled down ever' shade they was. I stretched out on the big couch in Doc's waitin' room, which was close't enough to hear any noise from the Doc an' his wife, even in my sleep.

I ain't never been as wore out in my life as I was that night. I went right off to sleep.

CHAPTER EIGHTEEN

Leonie Hempel

I was real glad when the bus come to Dallas. It was a hot old ride down there from Sulphide.

At the station I got down off the bus an' carried my suitcase an' the paper sack full of fried chicken I'd brung along inside. A lot of people was in there but I didn't see no Junior Knowles while I was lookin' around.

I was gonna set down in the waitin' room to wait on him like he said on the phone, when I seen old El Mercer, big as life, standin' over at the magazine stand a-lookin' at the pitchers on the books an' drinkin' a Coca-Cola. Jus' my luck! If there was jus' one man in the whole wide world I didn't wanta see, it was El Mercer.

To start with, El had allus drunk too much back home, an' iff'n he was drinkin' an' got to talkin' to you he'd talk yore ears off. You jus' couldn't git away from that man or make him shut up, neither. More'n once't he'd come 'twixt me an' my Junior, too. Allus a-takin' Junior off somewheres in that old car o' his where neither one of 'em never had no business a-goin'. They was allus inta somethin' t'gether. I couldn't stand El an' I didn't want him around, a-tall. An' Junior knowed how I hated El, so iff'n he sent that old fool to meet me at the station we was gonna have trouble right off, or my name wasn't Leonie Hempel.

Here, almost in the middle of Dallas, El didn't look no differ'nt than always. Dirty an' ragged, an' his nose red as a ripe tomater–from drinkin', I s'posed. Prob'ly had whiskey mixed inta that bottle he was a-nursin' on. I was all dressed up in my best. If he'd a-seen me an' started talkin' like he knowed me in front of all them town-folks I'd of died.

I'd a-gone up the stairs to where the restrooms was but I got to thinkin' what if Junior was to come in while I was hidin' in there. He might figger I missed the bus I come in on an' leave ag'in an' come back when another'n come in from Oklahoma. I was tryin' to make up my mind at the bottom of the stairs when I seen a policeman go up in back of old El an' tap him on the shoulder.

Goody! I reckoned Mister Mercer'd find out he couldn't git away with that stuff he pulled back home down here in a big city like Dallas. The policeman said somethin' to El an' then walked him over to a phone booth an' went inside. I reckon he was fixin' to call some more police to come take El to jail.

El stood outside the booth listenin' an' still suckin' on his Coca-Cola bottle. That's when I seen my Junior come in the door. Gosh, he shore looked handsome! All dressed up in a new blue suit an' wearin' a rainbow-colored necktie. He stood there just inside the door with that way of his, sorta lookin' down on ever'body like they was dirt, with his chin stuck 'way out an' them blue eyes a-flashin'. He needed him a shave, like allus, but anyhow I was thinkin' he was the best lookin' man in the whole wide world right then. I went towards him in a dead run.

"Junior!" I yelled.

He grinned real big at me an' shoved the white bundle he was carryin' up under his arm, so's he could tote my suitcase.

"There's my gal!" he said. An' he kissed me enough to make me know he meant it. Then he grabbed my arm an' we started out.

But old El had saw Junior an' he let out a drunken holler clean across the station.

"Good Lord! Keep that old fool away from us, Junior," I said. Junior give my arm a squeeze.

El was runnin' paddle-footed towards us an' when he come pretty close't Junior give him one o' his looks, an' I wondered why he stuck his hand inside o' his coat while he talked slow an' mean to El.

"Iff'n you don't git, I'll kill you!" he told El.

El didn't stop runnin' an' he didn't say nothin'. He jus' had a look on his face like he'd done lost his last friend, while he made a big circle 'round the station at a dead lope an' run out the door on the other side to where the busses come in. The policeman had come a-bustin' outta that phone booth an' pulled his pistol out an' was a-chasin' after El. He fired his pistol once't, up at the ceilin', 'fore he disappeared out the same doors El had went out.

"Le's git outta here, Leonie."

We went out the door an' got inta his car. It still had the motor runnin'—meanin' it was a good thing I never went to them restrooms—an' he drove off.

"Why you reckon that policeman was after old El so fast, Junior?"

"That El Mercer, he can git inta more dang trouble'n you can shake a stick at. I ain't got no idy what he done this here time."

"Way the policeman looked, if he catches El he'll wind up in a jail."

"S'pect so."

"Where'd you git this car, Junior?"

139

"Oh . . . down where I work at—b'longs to the comp'ny."

"You mean they give you a car to use?"

"Shore. Lookit, Leonie, you be gittin' yore clo'es outta yore suitcase an' stick this here bundle in."

"What in the world for, Junior?"

"Don't you start astin' questions, now. Jes' do it 'cause I said so."

I done like he told me. But there was still room for my new nightgown an' I put it back in, careful, in one end.

"Whatcha got in that sack, Leonie?"

"Jus' some chicken I fried an' brung along."

That made Junior grin—he shore loved chicken.

"Now you tell me what you got in the bundle in my suitcase you're so proud of, Junior."

He give me another grin.

"Reckon I hadn't oughtta tellya," he said, "but jes' take yourself a peek."

I opened it an' unrolled one corner of the bundle an' taken a look. Money! I looked further inta the bundle. It was plumb full o' money. When I had the corners folded back up I shut an' locked the suitcase an' set it on the floor of the car.

"Where'd you git it, Junior?"

He jus' laughed.

"B'longs to yore comp'ny, don't it, Junior?"

"Maybe-so."

"All right, then—don't tell me."

I was put out with him 'cause he wouldn't say, so I shut my mouth an' looked out the window. We was gittin' out on a highway, looked as if.

"Where we goin'?" I ast him.

"Iff'n I ain't mistaken, I ast you to come here an' git hitched. You forgit awready?"

140

"Oh, Junior! You mean that's where we're goin'? To git married?"

"I never meant nothin' else but."

Things was happenin' too fast for me. 'Fore I could git one thing figgered out somethin' else come up to mix me up.

"Junior, I'm real glad that's where we're goin'. . . . But iff'n you don't tell me where all that money come from I think I'm gonna bust."

He jus' laughed ag'in. Times, iff'n he wanted to, he could be the most aggravatin' man in the whole wide world—besides bein' the best lookin'! I felt like shakin' him.

Junior made such a quick right turn into a dirt road I was throwed over ag'in him. He stopped an' backed up an' got on the highway ag'in an' went back the way we had come.

"Whatcha doin', Junior? Forgit somethin?"

"Didn'tcha see them police cars an' policemen blockin' the road?"

"You mean that bunch way up yonder?" I pointed back.

"Uh-huh. Them. They ain't waitin' jest to kill time. They was waitin' for us. Good thing I seen 'em first."

"Us? Waitin' for us? You're in trouble, Junior, ain'tcha?"

"Sort of, I reckon."

"What'd you do? What sorta trouble?"

"Lookit, Leonie. You know I don't like lyin'—'specially to you. Iff'n I was to tell you what I done you wouldn't like that, neither. So it'd be better iff'n I don't tell you nothin' a-tall."

"But I wanta know! An' you gotta tell me, sometime. Might as well do it now, Junior."

"Maybe I gotta tell you sometime—but not now."

"Did you steal that money?"

"Sort of, I reckon. But I sort of earned it, too."

141

"That's mighty funny talk, Junior. All right. I'll quit astin' about it, an' then you'll prob'ly wanta tell me after while. Where we headed now?"

"I been tryin' to figger the same thing. If they's police on the highways, it's a cinch they're at the bus stations an' the depot. I think we better try the airport. They might not figger me to try an' git outta Dallas on a airplane."

"Junior, I gotta say somethin'. I know you're in trouble, an' I'll stick by you 'cause I love you—but I don't want to git in no trouble myself. I don't wanta wind up in no jail."

He slammed on the brakes an' skidded to a stop so quick I bumped my head ag'in the windshield.

"Git out, Leonie," he said. I looked at him an' started cryin'. I couldn't help it.

"I don't wanta git out."

"Iff'n you don't trust me, don't figger on goin' with me an' marryin' me!"

"I trust you, Junior."

"Then quit yore talkin' so much an' astin' me all them questions. I'm a-tryin' to think an' doin' my best to keep both of us outta trouble. Yore dang naggin' ain't helpin' none."

When he got in sight of the airport he turned into a dirt sideroad an' stopped under a clump of trees just off'n the road.

"We'll walk the rest of the way."

"Ain't somebody li'ble to take the car?" I ast.

"I reckon so."

"You stole it, along with the money, didn'tcha?"

"Shet up an' git outta the car!"

I did, an' he follered me, totin' the suitcase.

"Gimmie that sack of chicken," he said.

He opened up the sack an' stuck his hand in an' we walked up the road towards the airport. I was about scared outta my

142

skin, findin' out he done stole ever'thing he had. Not him. He jus' walked on up the road, eatin' on that piece o' chicken like he didn't care about nothin' in the whole wide world.

I cared an' was scared.

He must of done somethin' mighty, mighty mean to have policemen all over Dallas tryin' to catch him.

I was gonna hafta find out jes' what he done—as quick as ever I could.

CHAPTER NINETEEN

Bill Brown

By coming partially clean and unloading some of what I knew, I'd hoped to give the brainy Dallas detective a generous chunk of my headache. It didn't work. He left and the headache stayed, in all its glory.

But by giving him something to go on, maybe I'd steered him away from concentrating on me and checking on my past with L.A. Giving the devil his due, he had sure started the wheels turning, instead of just spinning.

The headache did ease off a bit though—after Kay finished spooning that hot broth into me and rubbed my temples deliciously with her fingers. I relaxed a bit. Even dozed again. I don't know how long, but not very. Unfortunately I woke up, and the little riveters were there again, pounding their needles into all the soft spots in my head. Kay was still there.

"Guess I dropped off. Was I out long?"

"Not long enough to do you much good. How do you feel?"

"So-so. Headache still with me, of course."

"Want an aspirin?"

"Not an aspirin . . . ten aspirins."

"One every hour. You're full of the stuff right now."

"Split the difference with me—make it eight."

"Here's one. Hold it 'til I get some fresh water."

"Miss Haas, it's . . . have you got any codeine?"

"No-o-o, I'm sure I don't. I'll see what's in my pill box." She fumbled in her purse a minute and grinned at me. "I have a Midol tablet."

"Give it here." I chewed it up along with the one lousy aspirin. The headache remained constant, like a bride of three days. I could hear Kay moving about the room while I held my eyes screwed together tight against the throbbing.

"I think I'll get up."

"You can't get up."

"Why not?"

"Stay down there and rest. You need it."

"Get me my clothes, Miss Haas."

I swung my feet from under the sheet. They must have been wired directly to a motor-driven pruning knife in my head. I slid to the floor on my knees and couldn't stand up. I crawled back into bed. Lying there felt mighty nice.

"Stay there, and rest. You need it," Kay said.

"You said that."

"You just proved it."

"I'll try again in a minute."

I looked at her face. She was beautiful—even with the black and blue mark on her temple leading into the corner of her eye.

She was lucky Junior hadn't killed her. But then, so was I. And I knew how lucky, because I couldn't remember crawling out of the car and into the bushes. Self-preservation in the subconscious, I guess. Kay had kidded me a little about being money-hungry because when they found me I had her purse

144

clutched in one hand. I didn't remember how I got that, either, but she said Junior had dumped me in the car on top of it.

I became engulfed in a wonderful, enchanting reverie. How nice it would to kill, torture, or even maim little Junior from Oklahoma. My smile must have been a beautiful thing as I tasted this over and over in all its possibilities.

"Why the happy face? Headache gone?" Kay asked.

"Why'd you interrupt?" I groaned. "I was just putting Junior through his paces in my mind. . . . Get me my clothes, will you?"

I tried again, this time just sitting up for a starter. My head peeled off like an airplane leaving a tight formation, buzzed the field, then settled down for a straight shot at the horizon. The ceiling cleared. I pushed the sheet off. Another milestone. Moving gingerly, I got my feet to the floor and sat on the edge of the bed.

They had really prepared me for comfort—I didn't even have shorts on. A bit of embarrassment trickled through the pain in my head when I realized Kay was sitting there watching me.

"Will you get me my clothes?"

"All right. I wanted to see if you could make it, that's all,"

Kay left the room. But the nurse came in, quick like a panther.

"Youcan'tgetupMr.Brown! YouhavetostayinbedMr.Brown!"

I pushed a hand through the air.

"Go get me an aspirin."

"It's too soon. You've taken too many, now. You get back in bed and stay there, do you hear?"

Snow White had better watch her step—the witch wasn't dead yet; not at all. She was disguised as a nurse.

"Nurse. I'm going to count three, and you'd better be gone. Or I'll do something I'll be sorry for the rest of my life—a

terrible thing. One. . . . Two. . . ." and the door closed behind
her fast retreat. I opened my eyes again. It was good not to
see her. I stood up, and danced a mad, uncontrollable tango
across the room to where Providence had placed a chair. I
landed in it.

Wow! A bit rocky. Quite a bit! I felt the bandage on my
head. Junior wasn't only strong under the arms; he wielded a
good pistol whip. And the pain in my groin as I staggered
across the room had told me he got results with his back-
kicks, too. I decided he wasn't a nice playmate.

Kay came back carrying my green gabardine suit and a
white sport shirt.

"It wasn't cleaned, but I had it sponged and pressed."

"I'll need shoes, too."

She pointed to them, under the bed. I remembered my buck-
and-wing across the room,

"Would you. . . ?" I waved vaguely at the shoes.

"Sure."

She brought them over to the chair and took a sock out of
each one.

She pulled the socks on for me. Then the shoes.

"What the hell," I thought. "If it doesn't bother her, why
me?" I was too weak to be conspicuously bothered, anyhow.

I found the shorts she'd brought with the suit and stepped
into them, getting up as I did so. Taking it easy, I balanced
myself into the pants of my suit. Then slid into the sport shirt.
I was beginning to feel a little more like a normal man with a
splitting headache. Back in the land of the living.

My mind began clicking on all at once again. Things to do.

"May I use your phone?" She brought it over and I sat
down with it. I dialed the operator and asked for Western
Union.

"Hello. Put me on with an operator . . . Hi. Take this message, please? To Ed Brown. Apartment 3C, 4125 Figueroa Street, L.A. . . . That's Los Angeles. Yes, that's what we call it out yonder in California–for short. Want the message? Okay, here goes . . . How are things on West Coast. Question mark. Clear comma or warmer. Question mark. Having a terrible time. Wish I was there. Rush answer care Western Union. All my love. Bill. Just sign it Bill . . . All right! The sender is Bill Brown, operator . . . What? . . . Oh. F – i - g - u - e - r - o - a. Yeah, odd. Think it comes from Mex. Now read me the wire, will you? . . . Fine. Very good . . . No, I appreciate your help-fulness, but I can't possibly cut this wire to ten words. Thanks. Charge it to this number and if I'm not here to receive the answer deliver it to this address."

She finally got the phone number and Kay's address right. I hung up, hoping I wouldn't have to send any more telegrams.

"Well, Miss Haas, guess I'd better get going and earn my retainer."

"You don't have to. Why don't you lie down and wait for news?"

"I'll rest better after I find Junior."

"Let Lieutenant Campbell find him. He refused our help."

"He's a little better cop than I figured, at that. But he can't recognize Junior–never saw him."

"We gave him a good description."

"It's not the same."

"He'll find him."

"I'll find him."

"Then we'll find him."

"You can lose lots of cars like that."

"There're still three in the garage."

"Okay. Let's go downstairs, one step at a time."

I stood up and fought the dizziness until it cleared. Then Kay helped me get as far as the bottom step. That stopped me. I sat down. Chimes sounded through the rooms.

"It's the door," she said. "I'll get it."

In walked the curious detective.

"We found your car, Miss Haas. One of the men is driving it over. Should be here, soon."

He spotted me resting on the steps.

"What got you out of bed, Brown?"

"Couldn't sleep, Lieutenant."

"Don't try to leave the house—you're still under arrest."

"I wouldn't think of it."

"You heard that, Miss Haas. He's in your charge and you're responsible for him when I want him."

"Thank you for your confidence. Where was my Cad?"

"In a motel, just as I thought we'd find it."

"Brilliant!" I murmured.

"Merely routine. As a matter of fact, it was reported by the motel's manager. Seems someone stole a blanket and left your Cadillac."

"Tsk, tsk," I put in. He got sore.

"Listen, Brown. I'm talking to Miss Haas here. No remarks from you are called for."

"Uh-huh. And how did they carry the blanket away? By motor boat, on foot, horseback, what? Did you ask?"

The detective laughed.

"That's the funny part. In a way, I mean. They left with some doctor, this manager says. The place was a mess—lots of blood. Funny part is the manager called the doctor but he can't remember what doctor it was, one of the doctors in the phone book, he says. With a Hudson, fairly old. He remembers that. Funny, huh?"

"Ha-ha!" I faked a laugh for him. "That is funny. Maybe he'd remember if you threatened to feed him the phone book. Ha-ha!"

"I've got a man on him. Routine. It'll come back to him." He turned his back on me. "Meanwhile, Miss Haas, we're running a check on all the doctors in town. We'll find him. The roadblock teams all have a description of the Hudson. Dark green, two-door sedan. That's about all we have at the moment. I wanted to keep you posted. Your car will be here soon."

"Thanks a lot, Lieutenant," I butted in again.

"You stay here, Brown. And quit trying to crack wise with me."

"Me?"

Miss Haas, as he so frequently referred to her, led him to the door and he left. She came back to where I was sitting.

"Why did you ride him so much?"

"Talking makes me forget the head. Almost. Well, Miss Haas, when your car gets here we'll take a drive and have a look for ourselves."

"Think it'll do any good?"

"I'm anxious to be of service to our brilliant protector."

"All right. Why wait? I'll bring another car around. . . . Oh, by the way, Bill, you may call me Kay."

"I can?"

"If you want to, I'd like it."

"Okay, Kay. You may call me Bill."

"Thanks, Bill."

"That's okay, Kay."

My God!

CHAPTER TWENTY

FRED CAMPBELL

When I got back to the car after leaving Miss Haas, my driver, Bob, was rolling a cigarette. That was one thing we had in common. Other than that he was a peaceful, happy driver and I was the butt of all the pranks of all the maniacs who dropped off in Dallas. I got in.

Bob blew a cloud of smoke at the window.

"Where to, Fred?"

"I'm not sure. Hold everything a minute."

That stupid motel manager. Couldn't remember what doctor he had called, but he could remember the laundry mark on the missing blanket and describe it like he had slept under it every night of his life. That's the world. Materialism. I hoped someday I'd have a case where everyone involved in any way would have a photographic memory.

Oh well, we'd find the doctor. Easy, but it would be slower. One doctor at a time to check in the city, and sooner or later there he would be. The next link in the chain. That is, if we didn't find him dead and the killers gone again. In that case, the next link was going to be tougher and we'd get farther and farther behind unless we got an unforeseen break. Well, one thing at a time. Police work is very simple.

"Let me make one, Bob."

He passed me the tobacco and papers. I listened to the radio calls as they flew back and forth while I rolled the cigarette and set fire to it. Several no makes on stolen cars. Some woman received a box through the mail and wanted a policeman to come out and open it. A disturbance in a beer joint on Commerce. On and on. Cops get all the troubles, big and little, in the end. I started to give Bob a gripe about this fact when the radio voice asked for me to come in. I picked up the mike.

"Campbell."

"A lead on the kidnappers, Lieutenant," the radio barked, "and it looks hot! A Doctor Mercedes claims to have one of them. Picked him up at a motel last night. Must be the one that's hurt. . . ."

"What's the address?"

"2358 Roseland Avenue. Repeat, 2358 Roseland Avenue. Dr. Paul E. Mercedes."

"On my way! I'll report in from there."

I stuck the mike back on the rack.

"Let's go, Bob!"

He threw in the siren and opened up the Buick. The siren made good interference, and in a few minutes we rolled up in front of the address. A sizeable crowd had gathered and one policeman was trying to stop their milling about and get them moved on about their business. But not them—they wanted to see! I jumped out and climbed the steps. It was an old frame building with the yard in very good shape. Flowers bordered the walk, and on the porch railing a few pots of pink geraniums were lined up. Somebody in the crowd recognized me.

"When you gonna catch them kidnappers, Fred? Me, I got the rope!"

The crowd laughed, and I smiled back at them, waved, and entered the house. The talk about a rope was supposed to be a joke, but there's many a red-neck moved to the city, and in cases like this there are more people than I like to admit who still consider hanging a fine means to an end.

Tommy Conover was on duty inside. A woman was prattling away in his ear, telling him all about it. I took her to be Mrs. Mercedes and it turned out she was. Tommy's expression said this wasn't the first time he'd had to listen to her story. I stopped over close to them, hiding a wink from her.

"Please tell me all about it, ma'am," I said.

She stopped the steady flow of gab, sailed at the chance of starting over, took a deep breath, and did so. She didn't give me much. It was probably the first night she'd ever spent in a closet and she still couldn't believe it. She reached the end of her brief tale and started over again with hardly a pause.

"Thanks a lot, Mrs. Mercedes. Tell Officer Conover here, now."

He threw me a look, and settled back.

"Where's the doctor?" I asked.

Tommy pointed, and I went into what looked like an operating room. Doctor Mercedes was there, working over some remains of the boy who had been literally chopped to pieces with a whip. From what I could see, I knew I wouldn't want to stay if all the bandages on his upper face were removed. The doctor glanced at me.

"Lieutenant Campbell, Homicide," I said.

He went back to work.

"I don't know why I'm doing this, Lieutenant—these places won't be noticeable in his coffin."

"He's dying?"

"No doubt of it."

"Suppose that's the reason he was left here?"

"Well, I don't know for sure. The other one was dead set on getting him treated and mentioned taking him with him once. Could be I convinced him the boy wasn't going to live, I don't know. That fellow was crazy, anyway, I think. Maybe he just changed his mind and didn't care any more."

"Maybe crazy some ways. Maybe like a fox, others, Doc."

"Could be he couldn't feel any pulse and left him for dead. It's the faintest sort of a beat—he'd need a stethoscope, or an awfully sensitive touch."

"Can I talk to this one before it's too late?"

"Sure. You can talk to him. You won't got an answer, though."

I lifted the pile of wet gauze covering the lower part of the boy's face. Jesus! I put it back.

"Lieutenant, who did this whipping?"

"Haas, himself—the kidnap victim's father. Quite a bad beating, wasn't it?"

"Worst I ever saw. I couldn't believe it."

"Haas was old school—law of the range and all that. Just in his blood."

"Eye-for-an-eye or not, that's a terrible thing, lying there," the doctor said.

"Haas is dead. Good thing, I guess. Wouldn't want this on my conscience. This kid didn't kill the girl, you know. Haas probably didn't have a conscience anyhow, though."

"It was the other one that did the dirty work?"

"Yeah, him. Did you get any hint of his intentions—like which way he might have planned to go?"

"No. . . . I don't think so. No."

I bent down over the boy. His breath had started coming in long, shuddering gasps and his jaw worked weakly, as though to get words out.

He died then.

It was eerie, seeing him go like that after looking for him so hard. I *would* find him in time for that. The doctor threw a sheet over him and lit his pipe.

"The whipping killed him. Right, Doc?"

"Well . . . depends, I'd say. That started it and was the cause, o'course. But I think he could've been saved with prompt and proper treatment and close attention—even when I first saw him. Lack of these results in shock and exposure—and the end."

"Can you say that on the certificate, Doc?"

"Don't see why not—that's my opinion."

"Well, that'll make it a little better for Haas' family – what's left of it."

"What's done's done. No use making it harder on the living ones," he said.

"Okay, Doc—thanks for seeing it that way. Looks like we're through, here. I'll send an ambulance and get the body cleared out of your way."

"Any time. I cancelled my appointments when I saw that mob out front."

"They'll break up. I'll leave a good man, in case Junior gets lonesome for his brother and comes back."

"I don't think he'll be back. He knew the end was near, I think."

"You can't predict a guy like him. I'll leave a man."

"Suit yourself, Lieutenant. And much obliged."

"Doc, do you think your wife can keep this quiet?"

"Do you?"

"Well, talk to her anyway, Doc."

"I'll try."

"Did he leave anything?"

"There's a nice leather bag—over there."

I went over and looked. Something clicked. A new leather bag, no, two of them just alike, were all we'd had to look for in the murder of that hustler in the hotel room downtown. It just might be. We could try to get an identification of the dead boy or his clothing out of that bartender in the grill where the Baeder girl made her last pickup. It was worth a try. And every little bit of pressure from upstairs I could get off my neck made my appetite that much better. Thinking back now over the descriptions of the customers with the identical leather bags I decided it was practically a cinch. Well, it would help.

I used the doctor's phone and called downtown. I ordered the ambulance for Donald, left instructions for the bartender to be called in when Donald's body got to the morgue, and was told the car's description had been broadcast after the Doc reported Junior had borrowed it. Then I called Miss Haas.

Miss Haas didn't answer. Neither did Mister Brown. Now what could I make of that? I thought of having a pickup put out on them with orders to book Brown for complete investigation. By God, I would!

I took up the phone, remembered a few things about Miss Haas, and hung up again halfway through the number I was dialing. Hell! Sure trouble if I did it, and probable trouble if I didn't.

I asked Mrs. Mercedes to join her husband in the other room, then talked to Tommy. I told him to stay in the house and set up a twenty-four hour guard outside, back and front; that I'd be in the car and expected to have Junior rounded up before dark so we could all start sleeping occasionally again. I left him sitting and waiting to listen to Mrs. Mercedes some more.

Bob was on the porch talking to the policeman who'd tried to reason with the crowd.

"Let's roll, Bob."

155

He got up, opened the car door for me, and I stepped in. The crowd was still thick along the sidewalk. I stepped out again and held up my hand for quiet.

"Folks, when I tell you the facts I know you'll be glad to go home. There isn't going to be any excitement here – I give you my word on that. I've ordered an ambulance to carry away a man who was injured. And that's all there'll be to it. By staying here now you will only worry the doctor and any patients who might want in. So let's all be reasonable and go home, what do you say?"

A few saw the light and drifted away, but I knew some of them would stay to see the ambulance load and drive off– mainly to be able to talk about seeing this and that, on the spot. Morbid curiosity. Well, why not? Kidnapping doesn't happen every day in Dallas. Thank God!

"All right, Bob. We'll make a round of the roadblocks, starting at the Fort Worth Pike."

Check. Check. Check. That's all there is to it. I sensed the old feeling of getting warm, and thought if Junior was still in Dallas I'd have him before the day was out. And I was pretty sure he was.

"Never mind the siren, Bob," I said. "Take your time."

Police work is simple.

Chapter Twenty-One

JUNIOR KNOWLES

The cold fried chicken shore hit the spot. I et three pieces while me an' Leonie walked up the road to the airport. I was watchin' things up there but I never let on to be a-worryin' none. Iff'n I done that she'd a-started them questions comin' at me ag'in.

They was a couple ol' busses an' maybe eight or nine cars settin' in the parkin' spaces in fronta the buildin'. Then I seen two of them cars was police cars.

"Whoa, Leonie," I said, an' taken holt of her arm.

"What, Junior?"

"Jest a minute—I gotta figger 'fore we git any clos'ter."

The ditch b'side the road was deep enough to hide in, settin' down. I pulled Leonie in an' set her down alongside o' me. Nobody couldn't see us in that tall grass even iff'n a car come by.

"Here's what, Leonie. You gotta go to that buildin' yonder an' see how many policemen is in there. How many an' where at."

"I don't see how that'll help any, Junior."

"We gotta git by 'em to git on the airplane, ain't we?"

"Junior," she said to me, "I don't go nowhere 'til you tell me about the money. I know you stole it, an' I want the gospel truth. I'm scared."

"You ain't got no call to be scairt, honey. Shore, I stole it. But it's done been done. No help for it."

"Oh, I jus' knowed it! You're in real terrible trouble, Junior! Where?"

"From a bank–that's all. They got a-plenty left."

"A bank! You robbed a bank, Junior? Lordy, mercy. . . . You was taught better, I know."

"Once't I git outta this here town o' Dallas, ain't nobody could find me. Now go on–"

"No! Cain'tcha see, Junior? God knows, I'd like to have money, too, but not this here money. It ain't right–it ain't our'n!"

"'Tis so–now."

"No it ain't. Now Junior, you gotta listen to me. You gotta give it back, an' ast the judge, or whoever, for mercy. It'll go easier on you than gittin' caught . . . an' I can wait some more, like I allus have. Why, maybe they wouldn't even send you to jail a-tall when the bank gits its money back. It's the only thing we can do . . . Junior . . . Junior–I don't wanta lose you. I love you–please do like I'm astin' you, honey."

She was talkin' crazy. But she thought she was a-makin' sense, I reckon. An' she was reely scairt. I only knowed one thing to do–scare her worse'n she awready was an' maybe it'd work. It's the only way I know to calm down a woman havin' a hissy.

I grabbed her shoulders an' shaken her good an' hard 'fore I turned her aloose.

"Now you listen to me a minute! You don't know ever'thing yet an' you're jes' babblin'. I ain't a-gonna give that there money back, an' iff'n you keep on spoutin' about it I'm gonna slap some sense inta yore head! Now, shet up about it!"

Now Leonie was a-bawlin', an' I knowed that meant she'd decide to do my biddin'. I knowed how to handle Leonie.

"Don't cry," I said. I hugged her up to me, tight. "Ever'thing's gonna come out all hunkydory, wait'n see."

After a little more blubberin' she slowed it down an' wiped her face on her pettycoat. She was pullin' herself t'gether a whole lots better.

"I'm all right, Junior. Whatcha want me to do?"

"I jes' wantcha to help—to do what I tellya we gotta do."

"Well. . . . All right, Junior."

She lean't over an' kissed me, but I never felt like doin' no sparkin' jes' then an' I shoved her off.

"Go on up to the buildin' an' see about them cops, first. An' then come back right here."

Her shoulders drooped an' she looked kinda sad, but she got up an' started down the road. I felt better—for a few minutes I'd sorta been leery o' what she might do, mixed up like she was. But now I figgered she'd do what I said from here on out.

She never stayed gone long. I'd jes' stood up in the ditch to look an' seen her comin' back. I waved at her an' set back down outta sight. She come inta the grass an' set b'side me.

"How many, Leonie?"

"All I could see was three, Junior. In uniform, I mean. How do we know all of 'em wear uniforms?"

"Where they at?"

"Well, one was by the door when I went in—a little man, nice-lookin', for a policeman. He had a little old red mustache, an'—"

"Dern his looks! Where's the rest?"

"I was jus' tellin' you what I—"

I give her a look.

"Well," she said, "the other two stayed pretty close t'gether, not far from the ticket-windows. An' one went over to a window twice't while I was there—watchin' the airplanes outside, I reckon."

"Three, huh? You shore?"

"That's all I seen."

"That's aplenty when you're talkin' about policemen."

Too dang many, I said to myself. But the roads had more'n that, an' by now they was lookin' for that doctor's car like zoo-monkeys lookin' for fleas.

"Leonie, here's some twenty dollar bills. Put 'em in yore purse an' go up there an' git two airplane tickets. To Houston."

"Houston?"

"Houston. Lots o' planes'll be goin' there. When you git 'em, find out what time we leave. An' then look around, or maybe the ticket man can tellya, an' see what door we go out to git to the plane. Iff'n he wants to know who them tickets are for, say Mr. and Mrs. George Smith—so's they won't know who we reely are. Now, say it back to me."

"I can remember. Git tickets to Houston, callin' us Mr. and Mrs. George Smith. Find out what time we leave an' the door we go out."

"That's right. But it ain't all. Here's the main thing—mosey around an' see iff'n I can git to where that door leads out 'thout no policemen a-seein' me. Look good, Leonie. You understand ever'thing now?"

"Yes, Junior."

"Awright. Light a shuck."

This was my only chance to git outta Dallas, with the roads all stopped up with cops. I put on a sweat waitin' on Leonie this time. But jes' so she done ever'thing the way I said an' learn't me a way to git out, I could wait till the cows come home.

She finally come back. She was smilin' when she set down ag'in.

160

"I made it easy, Junior. Got the tickets, an' we leave at one o'clock."

"The doors, how–"

"Lemmie finish. It's gate number seven. An' iff'n we walk on past the front door an' down to the baggage place, then go in through there, we come out in the hall right acrost from the right gate."

"No policemen in the baggage room?"

"No–not hardly nobody, when I went through."

"Anybody say anything when you got them two tickets?"

"Huh-uh. Not even the man I got 'em from. Jus' wrote down that name you give me."

"You done real good, Leonie. What time o' day is it now?"

"It was nearly ten when I got the tickets."

"Ten? Means we got three hours to wait, but it cain't be helped."

"How'll we know when it's time, Junior?"

"Dang if I know . . . but maybe they's a whistle that blows at noon somewheres around here. That'd give us a good idy when to start up there."

"That's smart, Junior."

"Anyhow, we better not wait here, I don't think. Better go back an' hide in them trees where I put the car. We can rest some–maybe I can git a little shut-eye. Shore ain't had much, lately."

Leonie follered me back to the car. I put the suitcase on the grass under the trees for a piller an' laid down. Leonie laid down b'side me. It was good, havin' her there. We snuggled up an' I kissed her. She kissed back real good–she was gonna make a wife worth havin' around. My heart was beatin' fast an' I knowed she was gittin' excited, too, lovin' each other up thataway.

"Leonie . . . I jes' thought o' somethin'. See iff'n that clock in the car's a-runnin', willya?"

She got up an' looked.

"It's tickin' away, Junior. It's a little after ten-thirty."

She laid back down an' we started all over, an' was feelin' fine—an' I was sorta feelin' Leonie, too. Then all of a sudden she set right straight up. Natcherly I bounced up right behind her.

"What didja hear, Leonie?"

"Nothin'. I jus' now thought about Donald. Where's he at, Junior? You wouldn't go off an' leave Donald here in Dallas —"

I couldn't talk about my brother or how bad I'd wanted to bring him with us.

"Is that all that's botherin' you? Donald's gone—taken his share o' the money an' left town awready. We split up, so's not to git caught. Don't worry none about Donald."

"He go on back home?"

"Now how could he? They'll look jes' as hard for us back home as in Dallas. He ain't never goin' back to Oklahoma, an' I ain't neither."

"That means I cain't go back neither. . . . Oh, Junior! I'm scared!"

She begin to cry, like all git out.

"Dang it, Leonie—don't go bein' scairt ag'in. I'm with you, ain't I? An' please don't cry no more, Leonie. C'mon an' lay down here by ol' Junior ag'in an' we'll jes' think about us— about what we'll do when we git to where we're a-goin'."

She quit her snifflin' an' stretched out by me ag'in, but I knowed she was still scairt, shakin' like she was.

"Leonie, I'm gonna buy you scads o' new clo'es, an' we'll go steppin' at them nice dancehalls all the time. You'll have the time o' yore life, honey. In all them big stores, buyin' anything you want. All kinds o' dresses an' shoes, an' bathin' suits–say, how 'bout a purty white bathin' suit? You'd shore look nice in it. How's that sound?"

"I don't want no white bathin' suit. . . ."

"Well, it ain't gotta be white–color don't make me no never mind, long as it's a bathin' suit an' it's on yore purty figger."

I could tell she was settlin' down some, an' I stroked her sweetlike to help it along, tryin' to take her mind off'n my troubles. Purty soon she was breathin' deep, ag'in my neck.

"It sounds nice, Junior . . . what else you gonna buy me?"

I knowed that was jes' to have somethin' to say 'cause she was scairt to let herself go. I jes' said, "Anything you see that you'd like to have," an' kept on a-rubbin' an' pattin' her back. She kept snugglin' harder an' harder ag'in me. I was drowsy an' let my eyes go shet.

"You sleepy, Leonie?"

She jes' give sort of a happy grunt an' said she wasn't.

"Well, iff'n I doze off a little, wouldja keep yore eye on the clock?"

"Uh-huh, Junior," she said, so low I nearly never heard it.

"Jes' think of what things you want, an' I'll git 'em for you in Houston, Leonie."

I shet my eyes. Leonie'd watch for me, I knowed. I got sleepier an' sleepier, an' then I reckon I was asleep, 'cause I was dreamin' I heard the twelve o'clock whistle an' me an' Leonie was on our way to git on a big airplane that'd git me outta this Dallas-town forever.

CHAPTER TWENTY-TWO

Bill Brown

From my lowly station at the bottom of the stairs I was watching Kay.

She was nice to watch. It might be a right pleasant permanent hobby.

I know I should stir my stumps, get the hell out into Greater Dallas and try to get a couple of hooks into my boy Junior. I had a hunch the pride of the force, Campbell, would get close, but that Junior would break away from him in the end. But at the moment I just didn't think I could make it.

My mind was floating on a haze of purple ectoplasm; and each time I moved my head the pruning knife would dig in and the little riveters would scream "That's far enough!" in sharp unison.

Some condition to be in.

I eased up from the stairs and crossed the hall to the bar. That was a brilliant crossing, but I made the zigs and zags come out even until I had a grip on the bar. Plenty of liquor in the bar, and as long as I felt like the granddaddy of all hangovers it might help to hitch the horse up to the front of the cart.

I downed a couple of good-sized hookers. No effect. I poured three fingers more, fat ones, in my glass. Kay came over.

"Is drinking going to do any good?"

"Nothing could do me any good. And vice versa–meaning me either."

164

I chewed up the three fat fingers. Same thing. No effect.

"I don't think you'd better drink any more."

"It's your whiskey."

"I didn't mean that."

"Well, what did you mean?"

"I meant drinking wouldn't help you."

"Are we going through that again?"

"Bill. Please."

"Please? Pour you one, you mean?"

"Please don't drink any more!"

I fumbled around and found a cigarette.

"May I smoke?"

"You're trying to be hateful."

"It's customary to ask a lady, isn't it?"

"Yes. . . . You may smoke, Bill."

I lit the cigarette. I was sore at myself and taking it out on this poor little rich girl. She wasn't a bad kid. Plenty on the ball, considering everything she'd had to take on the chin.

"I'm sorry, Kay. I don't feel so good. Don't pay any attention."

I set the glass down on the bar.

"I know, Bill." She smiled at me sweetly. A martyr. She squeezed my arm, lovingly. Then the phone rang and she walked over to answer it.

"Hello? All right, I'll take it," she said.

She nodded once, twice, thanked whoever it was, and racked the phone.

"It was a telegram for you, Bill."

"It was? Too bad I wasn't here to take it."

"I took it for you. I thought with your head and all–"

"Thanks. Would it bear repeating? Or do you think with my head and all–?"

"It didn't make any sense to me–"

165

"It wasn't sent to you."

"It was from Ed Brown, Los Angeles." Her forehead wrinkled and she closed her eyes. "'All is forgiven. Traffic is heavy. Love. Love. Love. Ed.'"

Kay sent me a question-mark look.

"Isn't that silly? What's forgiven? Trouble with a woman, maybe?" she asked.

It made a lot of sense to me. The short-cutting brother. Deciphered, it meant I was still on the force. The heavy traffic– I was free to go back and manipulate it, turning with the signals again. That last hot day was a long, long time ago. How long was it? Let's see . . . actually, less than a week! Jesus.

Anyhow, that telegram sounded good to me. Somebody had covered for me. Something had been worked for a whitewash. I didn't know what it could be. Ed could have hinted, in the place of the 'love, love, love'. But it didn't matter–what I did now was the thing that mattered. All that repeated love from Ed just meant he wasn't going to be cheated out of his full limit of words for the rate he paid.

"What does it mean?" Kay asked.

"They're cutting my vacation short–in L. A. Want me back on the job."

"You're not going, are you?"

"Sure–why not?"

"There's a job here. Remember?"

"Uh-huh, I remember. Even with my head."

"And when we finish this job, Bill, I'll get you another one. Right here in Dallas."

"God forb–we, huh? That sounds good. Also, another job sounds pleasant. I can't wait."

I drained the glass without moving my head more than I had to, and dropped the butt I'd been dragging on into it.

"Is that meant to be sarcastic? I can't tell what you mean half the time," she said.

"Maybe I'd better finish the first job first. Before we settle my future."

"Where do we start?"

"I start by talking to that doctor who had Donald. The dazzling Lieutenant could've missed a load there, maybe."

"I'm ready."

"Not me. I need another gun. I loaned mine out."

Kay crooked her finger and I followed her, steadying myself against the wall, into the library. I wasn't anxious to see that room, but if she could take it I could. It had been well cleaned. She opened a wall-case full of pistols, shotguns, rifles, and a scattering of knives.

"Weapons were . . . Dad's . . . hobby."

"Yeah?"

I picked out a .38 Police Special. I like 'em. I checked it to see if it was loaded. It was. I wouldn't know why, in a trophy case like that, but it was.

"Nice collection—and ready," I said. "Do we wait for the Cad? Or didn't you mention a bevy of cars stored away somewhere?"

"Why wait? Let's take my Jaguar. They're fast cars."

"You can say that again. Junior could want a race, too, if we catch up to him."

She went for the Jaguar and I went out the front door to wait. It was getting to be a habit. I sat down on the front steps. I would have given my soul and something to boot for just twenty-four undisturbed hours in a bed. Would have, I mean, if my time wasn't leased to the L. A. Police Department.

Kay brought a dustcloud with her as she swung the little English car through the gravel drive and slid up in front of the porch. It was slick as a wet seal. A California seal. So was

Kay. I got in, but I wasn't too comfortable. It wasn't built for sedentary workers of my bulk. But there was room to make it.

"Do you know where to go?" I said.

"I'm driving, am I not?"

"You're driving."

I must have made a picture. Somewhat more than two hundred pounds of beef with a white bandage around the top of my head like a turban, sticking out of a red, midget car. Oh, well.

We knew the doctor's house before we saw the number. A goodly crowd was there. We pulled up behind a police car parked in front and the crowd turned, gave us a thorough once-over and started arguing about who we were. They looked like a flock of sheep who didn't know if they were getting a ram or a goat.

Kay ordered the uniformed policeman over to the car. More and more she was registering as the imperious type. Maybe I would be too if I had more money than a firm of public accountants could account for.

"Is Lieutenant Campbell here?" she asked the guy.

He ogled her beauty and said, "No, ma'am. He left a while back."

"We want to see the doctor, then."

"Sorry, ma'am. Him and his wife ain't talkin'. The Lieutenant's orders—"

"I want him to look at my head," I said.

"He ain't seein' no patients, neither. Sorry."

"Thank you," Kay told him.

A siren came down the street and the crowd stretched rubber necks. The hearse. It stopped at the curb, two men got out, took a stretcher from the back doors, and went into the house.

"Let's go," I said.

168

"Wait a minute."

The stretcher bearers brought out a covered body and placed it in the back of the hearse. They drove away, not bothering to turn on the siren.

Donald didn't have a chance, I thought. This would be with me a long time. A full-grown cop, walking out on a plain, premeditated, vengeful murder.

"I'll be right back," Kay told me.

She got out and went into the house. I smoked a cigarette, and she came right back as she'd promised. She got in and drove away.

"All right, I give up. What'd you find out?" I asked.

"Where the Lieutenant is. I want to check with him for the latest."

"And where is 'brains'?"

"Out on the Shreveport highway."

"Better drop me a block this side, or he won't like you no more."

"I'll handle it."

The shock must be wearing off—there was that sharp tone again. As if when she cracked the whip Dallas would have to jump through a hoop. I'd seen enough whipcracking. I filed it away just under a knifeblade in my head.

The fresh air felt good on my face at least. There was plenty of it, the way she kept jamming her toe down on the accelerator. We got to the roadblock too fast to suit me. Campbell's car was there. He leaped out of it and rushed over.

"You, Brown! I left you under arrest—told you to stay in."

"So you did. But my jailer was leaving. I'm with my jailer— what do you want? Egg in your beer?"

Kay started handling it.

"It's perfectly all right, Lieutenant. Don't raise your voice so. Mr. Brown has a headache."

169

"I'll cure it for him. I've had about all of his headache excuses I want."

"Got an aspirin on you, Lieutenant?" I asked.

His face was a deep red. He started the explosion, but the look on Kay's face or the yell from his driver stopped him—I didn't know which, but would have put my money on Kay's look.

"Fred! Fred!" his driver was calling. "I think you better hear this. It's the airport . . . Love Field."

The Lieutenant wheeled and walked to his car. He wasn't on the radio long, and I couldn't hear a thing he said. He shouted at Kay from his car:

"Take Brown back to your place and keep him there, or I'll lock him in jail so deep he'll need a steam shovel to dig his way out."

He said something to his driver and the Buick roared away. Kay turned to look at me.

"Well?" she said.

"He's latched onto something," I said.

"Think so?"

"Didn't you see how brave he got? Almost insubordinate."

"Well, where to? Home?"

"Later, maybe. The airport, first."

"You think it was a report on Junior?"

"I wouldn't be surprised. Not in the least."

"Let's go, then," she said.

I couldn't be absolutely sure because we were going so fast, but I thought Lieutenant Campbell's face turned awfully red again as we went around his Buick on the way to the airport.

CHAPTER TWENTY-THREE

Leonie Hempel

Junior dropped off an' started snorin'. Layin' there with him, I was tryin' to think about buyin' things down at Houston, like he told me, but I couldn't keep my mind to it. There was oodles o' things I'd like to of had, but what good would they do me?

What good would purty clo'es, shoes an' permanent waves do me when I was a-setting in jail or a prison-house for women, looking outta windows with bars acrost? Iff'n I was to help Junior git past them policemen an' git away, I'd be in 'most as much trouble as him. I've saw it in the pitcher shows an' girls doin' what I was doin' git a name—ever' time. I'd be a gun-moll, that's what! Me that no policeman'd never spoke to, 'ceptin' to say 'howdy'!

I reckoned I wouldn't be treated as bad as Junior, but I knowed it'd be awful jus' the same. Ever since Junior first started a-courtin' me, Mama an' Papa allus told me he'd wind up in jail someday. I hadn't never believed it, but he was a-gittin' mighty close to it right now—an' takin' me along with him, too.

He laid there propped ag'in the suitcase, peaceful as a jus'-born lamb, sweat pourin' outta his face. There wasn't no breeze a-tall an' it was so hot his shirt was gittin' wet under his coat. Ever'thing was quiet, an' over where the shade from

171

them trees stopped the heat was a-makin' the air just off'n the ground look wavy.

The hair right next to his head was a little darker than the rest, 'cause his head had sweat some, too. He looked so sweet, sleepin', an' I loved him with all my heart. I didn't care 'bout all that money—I mean, I didn't care 'bout it iff'n it'd git us both in prison. I jus' wanted plain old Junior, 'thout no trouble or takin' all them chances. Jus' like he was an' forever. Not for just a few days 'fore they put us both in differ'nt jails—where we couldn't even see each other an' where we'd be lookin' forward to years of wishin' ever'thing had a-been differ'nt.

Iff'n Junior'd only do like I ast him! The judge might have mercy an' not be too hard on him iff'n he was honest enough to take the money back to the bank an' own up to doin' wrong. He might go to jail, but iff'n he was good he could git out sooner; an' I could wait on him, just like I'd been a-doin' most o' my life.

Iff'n I helped him an' he could git away this time it wouldn't do no real good. They wouldn't quit a-lookin', not never. They'd track us down like sheep-killin' dogs. Even iff'n they didn't find us for a spell, most o' that money'd git spent while we was runnin' an' hidin', runnin' an' hidin'. Then Junior'd figger he had to git us some more an' most likely he'd try robbin' somebody else! An' it'd go on an' on an' on, gittin' worse an' worse, till we was in jail.

It's better not to start a-runnin' in the first place, 'cause the road jus' don't have no end once't you start. How in the whole wide world was I gonna git Junior to believe that? He wouldn't listen to me no more, not in seven hunderd years, would he. There was only one thing for me to do iff'n he was dead set ag'in savin' hisself from such a terrible end.

I'd hafta do it for him. I loved him too much to let him git in such a mess, even iff'n he might hate me for takin' it on myself to git him out. Once't I got my mind made up it wasn't hard a-tall.

I lifted his head up real easy an' slid the suitcase out from under it a little at a time. Then I let his head back down on the grass careful an' gentle an' he kept on a-snorin' slow an' soft. I tiptoed out to the road with the suitcase full o' money.

Once't outta them trees I lit out a-runnin' hard as I could for the airport. I didn't look back till I got to the door. When I did Junior wasn't follerin' me so I knowed he hadn't woke up. I don't know what he'd of done to me iff'n he caught me 'fore I got there.

I went in the front door an' stopped to catch my breath an' think about what I had to do. It still wasn't too late—I could still go back an' run away with Junior for the rest o' my life. Tears was rollin' down my face an' my heart was achin' like a sore tooth. The ways of a woman are hard. Like that song, "You allus hurt the one you love." A woman ought not to hafta make big decidin's for other people, but it nearly allus falls to a woman to do, looks as if.

I knowed I was doin' the right thing but that didn't make it no easier. Some folks was a-lookin' at me kinda funny-like, so I tried to quit cryin'. I wiped the tears off'n my face with the back of my hand and marched right up to the policeman with the little red mustache.

"I want to talk to the Chief o' Police," I said.

"I don't doubt it, lady. Lots of people do. But it's like this—these airlines charge just so much and they figure if you don't like it you can travel some other way. The chief himself can't make it no cheaper."

He walked away from me an' left me a-standin'. He must've thought I wanted to argy about ticket prices. The man at the information window was countin' up figgers on a addin' machine an' I waited on him to git finished.

"Yes, ma'am?" he said.

I didn't know jus' how to start.

"I got some real important information," I said, "but I won't tell it to nobody but the Chief of Police."

"Yes, ma'am."

"It's real important."

"Yes, ma'am; I'm sure it is."

"Would you git him on the phone for me?"

"I'd rather not."

"But it's real important!"

"Well, look, lady, wouldn't you talk to one of the policemen over there? They'll help you, or if they can't they'd be glad to call downtown for you."

"All right, but—"

He hollered at the policeman I'd just got through talkin' to, an' he come towards us with a sour look on his face like he had a bad taste in his mouth.

"This little lady has a problem," said the information man. "Will you help her out?"

"Gladly," the policeman said, turnin' to look at me ag'in. "What can I do for you, Miss?"

"Y'all are lookin' for the man that robbed the bank—and I know where he is!" I said, real fast, an' then I broke down cryin' ag'in. I'd said it now an' it was too late to take it back. He taken my suitcase an' led me over to a bench an' set me down. He was real nice an' started pattin' me on the shoulder an' tellin' me not to cry, but I couldn't help it.

"I want to talk to the Chief of Police."

He called another policeman over. I stopped cryin' now an' I was bound an' determined I wouldn't break down no more. But I wasn't a-goin' to turn Junior over to no ever'day

174

policemen. I was gonna make a deal where Junior wouldn't git hurt or killed. Either they'd do it my way or I wouldn't tell 'em nothin' a-tall.

They walked a few steps away an' talked to each other. Then they come back an' wasn't neither one smilin'. The tall one talked to me first.

"What bank was it that was robbed, ma'am?"

"I don't know."

"But you know who robbed it?"

"I reckon I do—I'm gonna marry him."

His eyes opened wider an' he looked s'prised.

"Well, where is he now?"

"I ain't sayin'. I don't want him hurt none, an' I wanta make a swap to be sure he ain't. I ain't tellin' y'all, 'cause y'all don't have no right to make no swap with me. I wanta talk to one o' yore high-up bosses."

They didn't like me sayin' that, I don't think.

"You're right about us," he said, "but you're wrong about our bosses, too. The police in Dallas don't make deals—high up or not. But you could be arrested yourself—for obstructing justice."

"Don't scare her, Marvin," said the one with the red mustache.

"He ain't scarin' me! Not a bit. I may be from Oklahoma an' the country, but I know a little bit. I won't talk to nobody but the Chief of Police, scairt or not."

"All right, lady, all right. But we've got to know you're tellin' the truth. We can't get the chief out here on a wild-goose chase."

"I can prove it. Don't you worry none."

"How?"

"With what's in my suitcase—take a look, iff'n you doubt it."

He opened it up.

"Holy Christ!" was what he said.

They taken a good look at the money an' then the one with the red mustache lit out the front door like Satan was after him. The tall one shut the suitcase an' took me by the arm an' started for the door.

"You've made me a very happy man," he said.

Well, I didn't know why he was so happy. I wasn't happy a-tall, an' I knowed Junior was gonna be awful unhappy 'bout ever'thing.

The happy policeman taken me to a police car outside. Inside the car a radio was blastin' away an' the red-mustached one was talkin' into it, with somebody else talkin' back at him at the same time.

I reckoned we'd git a little action, now.

CHAPTER TWENTY-FOUR

Junior Knowles

Dreamin' about that twelve-o'clock whistle musta woke me up. An' it was so hot I was smotherin'.

The leaves hangin' over me in the trees was gray from the dust settled on 'em an' they wasn't no breeze to shake 'em, not none. I stretched out my arms an' then–the suitcase wasn't there!

I come straight up an' looked ever whichaway. Gone! Leonie, too! No Leonie an' no suitcase! It was then it come to me the twelve-o'clock whistle wasn't no twelve-o'clock whistle, a-tall. It was a sireen, an' it was comin' clos'ter an' clos'ter!

I run behind a tree to watch. A police car whanged past wide-open, sireen a-screamin' bloody murder, an' went right on up the road tords the airport. Them fellers meant bizness, an' it made my breath sorta stick in my throat. At first I felt like lightin' out runnin' somewheres–anywheres. But I ain't one to be scairt for long. I hadta hold myself on a tight rein, now, for shore.

Leonie an' the money both bein' gone meant they musta went t'gether. Of course! Any fool could see that. I shore hated to think it but it was bound to be. From there it wasn't hard to figger out.

When things happen they happen an' ain't no livin' man can undo or do 'em differ'nt once't they're did. It was my own fault, my own dern fault! Thinkin' back, I knowed I

177

shoulda saw it comin'. I reckon I had saw it an' jes' shet my fool eyes to it. I was so tuckered out an' so close to gittin' outta Dallas I'd jes' went along—coastin', so's to speak. Not givin' Leonie credit for bein' a woman, when all the time I shoulda been rememberin' it. That's all she was—jest a woman.

A woman ain't nowheres near like a man an' can't think straight like a man. They allus gotta do somethin' 'thout thinkin' it out ahead time. That musta been Leonie's trouble, too. She was prob'ly sorry right now. Prob'ly had told herself she was a-helpin' me out. Didn't make no differ'nce what she told herself now. It was did, an' too dang late to be sorry for me.

Wakin' me up was one time a sireen had did some good, anyhow. Now I could git away. Dang good thing that bunch o' cops never drove up quiet. They'da got me like a baby in his cradle. Now I hadta move, fast, an' they wouldn't never git me.

I looked at the Doc's car. Naw. Iff'n I taken it ever cop in Texas'd know it was me a-drivin' it. Best let it set. Then they'd hafta wonder iff'n I'd stole another car or walked, or how I was a-gittin' around.

Them cops'd figger me to light a shuck tords town an' try an' git some other kind o' ride outta town. So I started a-runnin' the other way down the dirt road tords the country. I'd git in somebody's house an' hide, till night come, anyways.

Iff'n they started lookin' in all the houses around here I'd think of somethin' else. They jes' might do that, too, I figgered. Ain't smart to think cops're too dumb.

Wasn't but one of me ag'in all of them, but iff'n I could ever git outta Dallas I'd be long gone. No cops wouldn't never git me then. Lucky they was some loose money in my pockets when Leonie robbed me. Had about a season's laborin' wages, at least. An' I had me a plan that might fool them cops, even givin' 'em credit for bein' smart.

I still had them tickets Leonie had got. I could hole up in some house till the sun went down. Then I'd work my way back to the airport an' see iff'n I couldn't use one o' them tickets. That'd shore be the last thing they'd 'spect, so natcherly it was the best thing to do.

I had a good head start on 'em now, so I slowed myself down an' jes' walked. Might need my wind later on in case I got in a hurry ag'in. I went right on by the first house I come to. They'd be shore to check the first house or two away from the car. 'Bout half a mile on down the road I come to this house settin' back a piece from the road, with a big ol' scraggly hedge 'twixt the yard an' the road. That'd do.

I went in at the gate an' crossed the yard an' clumb a few steps to the gallery. I banged on the door with my fist an' waited, an' then banged ag'in.

Shore be lucky if nobody wasn't home.

But a old woman 'bout fifty opened the door. The screen was hooked when I tried to pull it open.

"What d'you want, boy? I was takin' my nap!" she whined out at me.

"I'm awful sorry, ma'am. It's mighty dry, a-walkin' in this here sun. Wanted to ast iff'n I could git a glass o' water."

"It's too hot for a body to be walkin' today."

"Yes, ma'am, it shore is. Iff'n I didn't hafta git back to Fort Worth I'd jes' curl up somewheres in the shade, myself."

I figgered on gabbin' with the ol' woman till she got the screen open. I coulda broke the hook, but I never wanted to scare her 'less'n she made me.

"Dallas is bad enough," she said, "but if you're from Fort Worth I don't have to tell you about heat an' hot weather."

"No, ma'am. Cowtown does git mighty warm, at times."

"Warm! Why, Dallas is cool beside Fort Worth."

"Reckon so, ma'am . . . but I could shore use that there drink."

"Oh, excuse me, you poor man! You come right on in and I'll fix some icewater."

"Don't go to no trouble—"

"No trouble a-tall—just come on in and I'll fix it in a jiffy."

She unhooked the screen an' went tords the back.

I shet the big wood door, locked it, an' pulled my gun out. I caught her 'fore she got to the kitchen an' shoved the gun in her back. She turned an' seen the gun. She let out a mousy squeak an' dropped on the floor like a bundle o' rags.

I found a closet an' drug her to it an' shoved her in.

"That's a dang good place to finish yore nap," I said, but she never heard me a-joshin' her. After lockin' her in I taken a look at the rest of the house.

It was a big two-story one. Six rooms downstairs an' four up, not countin' bathrooms. I locked all the windows an' doors an' pulled all the shades down. Then I picked out a window upstairs where I could see all o' the front yard an' the road a piece both ways. A side window in the same room gimmie a look at most o' the back, the chicken houses an' on out to the fields. A fence was built from the chicken yard out to the hedge that run along the road.

Iff'n I had to make a run for it I might could make the chicken yard 'thout too much danger o' somebody seein' me— iff'n they come after me from the front like I 'spected. Then I could belly along behind the weeds a-growin' down the fence-row till I come to the hedge, an' git from there inta the ditch. I could crawl in the ditch to some trees 'bout fifty yards back up the road.

They was a lot of 'ifs' in my thinkin' 'bout how to git away. I never had too good of a spot, awright, but I figgered I had a good chance't. An' maybe they wouldn't even think to look in all the houses. Anyhow, they wasn't nobody in sight a-comin' up the road yet, so I went back downstairs.

I pushed the settee an' some chairs up ag'in the front door an' moved a big table in the kitchen over ag'in the back door. Iff'n they only come one way that'd slow 'em down till I could git out another way. I looked in the icebox an' made me a lairpin' good sandwich outta some baloney an' onions an' tomaters. I washed it down with a pitcher o' milk that was good an' cold. I made me two more o' them sandwiches an' taken 'em up to my lookin'-out window, an' set 'em handy on the window sill. I set down in a chair an' started waitin' an' watchin'.

I was feelin' purty good now. I'd shore got around some, the last coupla days. But I was a-gittin' fat on it. More excitement than I'd saw in my whole life in Oklahoma, an' I was a-lookin' for'd to some more in a dang short time. I'd got to wheres I sorta craved it, like a cat goin' after catnip. My name was startin' to be knowed now, I reckoned.

Folks back to home might awready be a-readin' 'bout me or hearin' o' my doin's on their radios. Kept on thisaway, I'd prob'ly be ahead o' Purty Boy Floyd. No tellin' how famous I'd git to be. An' I hadn't never even figgered on it, a-tall.

Jes' one o' them lucky spells what come along once't in a lifetime. But most folks gittin' sech a break don't have enough gumption to grab a-holt an' make the most of it.

One thing, nobody'd never take Junior Knowles alive, neither. Not with my rappitation. I started a-laughin' out loud.

In about six or seven hours, iff'n my luck helt out, I'd be a-landin' down in Houston. An' I figgered to have some more fun an' make me some more easy money down thataway. Maybe my name would git to be knowed in Houston good as in Dallas. But I was gonna work it differ'nt in Houston.

From here on out I'd be workin' by myself. No more dang fools or women-folks was gonna git in my way. Lone wolfer, that's what. I'd git even for Donald. An' Leonie. Somebody'd pay for all them things that went wrong in Dallas.

I wondered iff'n they'd caught El yet. He'd git caught for shore an' stretch a rope. Wasn't for him I'd be outta here an' in Houston or Noo Orleens or someplace awready. He shore had made me mad, actin' sech a derned ol' fool. Well, it was too late for me to help him or hurt him, no matter where he'd got to. Let 'em hang him—he'd done lived 'bout as long as me an' Donald both put t'gether, anyways. He never had no complainin' a-comin', but iff'n I knowed El he'd do plenty complainin', awright. Wouldn't doubt but what he'd try blamin' me, too—right up to the last kick in his big feet. I laughed ag'in.

They got ever'body now but Junior, I thought. Iff'n they ever got close't enough to git me, they'd be a-hollerin' for somebody to help 'em turn me a-loose. I checked my gun, an' broke a hole in the screen so's I could shoot through it easy. Iff'n I went I'd shore take some company along with me.

I was still sorta sleepy but I fit it off. Junior Knowles had done slept his last wink in Dallas, 'cause ever' time I shet my eyes I got clos'ter to my coffin. I started nibblin' on one of the sandwiches. I thought about a Coca-Cola I'd saw settin' in the icebox, an' went back down an' got it. I was back at my chair a-sippin' the coke when I seen the police car creepin' along the road.

It come inch by inch, like a big snail, an' they was a man standin' on the runnin' board. Him an' the driver was both cops. They musta been a'lookin' in the ditch on both sides for me. Well, I wasn't in no ditch—they coulda saved theirselfs the trouble.

182

Then I seen a li'l ol' car a-follerin' 'em along, jest as slow as they was goin', an' about as far behind the police car as I coulda throwed a middle-sized brickbat. Two people was in it, too, but I never figgered they was policemen. Two was all that li'l ol' toy car would hold, an' I had me a hunch who them two'd turn out to be. Then the police car stopped—in fronta the house!

The driver clumb out, holdin' a gun in his right hand. He come to the gate an' stopped, an' I seen he had a li'l red mustache.

"Hey! Hey, in the house!" the fool yelled. "Anybody at home?"

We was at home, awright, but I never told him so. Even with that red mustache Leonie'd thought was so dern cute, I still hoped he'd go on about his bizness a-lookin' for me—somewheres else. But he wasn't that smart, the pore fool.

"Cover me, Marv—I'm gonna check the house," he hollered at his pardner.

He got the gate open an' started walkin' onta the grass. I taken good aim. Don't usually bother 'bout aimin, but I wanted to be shore not to have no hurt cops a-crawlin' around in that hedge with guns in their hands jes' now. I squeezed the trigger slow, an' caught him jes' where I'd been a-lookin' – square-dab in the middle o' the chest. He wouldn't be doin' no crawlin'. He wouldn't even know he hit the ground, he was so dead. The bullet had sorta balanced him in the middle of a step for a second, then he toppled onta his belly, showin' me a big wet sticky-lookin' spot in the middle of his back.

His pardner musta saw it, too, I reckon. He was under the wheel an' had that car in high in less'n ten yards. He never had to be in sech a hurry—not long as he was goin' away from me—'cause I wasn't gonna waste no shots. Mine was ever' one gonna be for keeps.

I looked up the other way, where the li'l toy car had stopped b'side the road. A man an' woman had got out an' was a-watchin' the house. So now I could git on with the plan I'd worked out—this here place would most likely be swarmin' like a beehive 'fore long. I laughed out loud. Looked as iff'n my luck was still a-holdin'.

Right now I meant to find out. The man an' woman was still standin' in the road gabbin' when I left the window an' headed for the back door of the house.

CHAPTER TWENTY-FIVE

Bill Brown

The Lieutenant's driver must have found some extra space between his foot and the floorboard after we went around him. When we got to the airport and Kay stopped at the entrance, I heard their siren screaming for a clear road not far behind us.

"Stay in the car, Kay," I said.

"Why?"

"I just think it's best."

A pair of police cars were in front of the entrance. Two cops were standing by the cars with a girl between them. The cops looked as if they'd just been informed of joint ownership in a winning sweepstakes ticket. But the girl's face was anything but happy.

She was a pale creature, rather slight but well-proportioned, generously freckled, and crowned with a mass of dark red hair. She had evidently been crying but appeared calm enough

184

now, even if a bit dazed. Two cops and one mad girl didn't add up to anything but three, for me.

"Wonder who she is?" Kay brought out.

"I wouldn't know. Pretty, isn't she?"

"Too thin."

The siren drifted from shrill to guttural tone and died entirely as Campbell's car pulled up beside us. He was on the ground before it stopped rolling.

"You two will stay in your car and not interfere in this," he said.

"We're helping you," Kay said.

I didn't say anything, but I noticed the red flush wasn't quite gone from his face.

Campbell held a conference with the cops and the girl. She talked a blue streak, and he was being mighty nice and polite to her. He went so far as to pat her gently on the head once. I'd have given a plugged quarter to hear what she was saying, but it didn't carry.

He got into his car, with the girl sitting in the front seat beside him, and used the radio.

"Kay, you'd better have him tell you what's up."

She went over and talked to him a minute and came back.

"You'd never guess. It's Junior's girl friend. She's turned him in and agreed to take the Lieutenant to his hiding place. Nice girl friend!"

"I'll be damned! He's even managed to work in a love affair! He gets around."

"Let's follow along."

"Naturally—we want to help the 'brains' all we can."

The Lieutenant pulled out, sans the siren, and we trailed him. A half-mile down the highway toward town they turned into a dirt side-road and stopped near a clump of trees. We stopped behind his car.

Campbell and his driver went into the trees with their guns ready, and we could see them stalking an old green car parked in the middle of a grassy patch under the trees. Then they started going over the ground closely, all through the trees. Nothing happened.

"That must be the Doctor's car," Kay deduced aloud.

"Wait here," I said.

I climbed out of the midget with some difficulty and joined the Lieutenant.

"Did he skip?" I asked.

"Yeah. Couldn't have been gone long. But he's gone."

"Sirens are funny that way—they make some people move awfully fast."

That drew me a long, dirty look before he said anything else.

"He probably hitched a ride back towards town on the highway. Then again, he could've gone down this road." He pointed down the sandy lane.

One of the police cars from the airport pulled up and stopped.

"Marvin!" the Lieutenant called. "You and Harry go down this road and check each house. And the ditches on each side. No use going over three or four miles—he can't be far. I'll check the other way and keep the radio hot to get a real hunt started. We'll comb this whole end of the county, if we have to. Contact me if you hit on something."

"Yes, sir," said Marvin.

"Bob, call in and get more men out to the airport. Get the whole damn field surrounded."

"Yes, sir," Bob said, and got busy on the radio.

My respect for the Dallas homicide officer took another upward curve.

"Lieutenant," I said, "do you mind if Miss Haas and I follow along behind Marvin there?"

"Does it make any difference whether I do or not?"

"I just thought I'd ask–"

"Go ahead. It's probably safe enough–I think Junior went the other way."

I went back to the Jaguar and Kay, telling myself he could be right. But if my hunch about the siren-scare had scored, he could've gone the other way just as well. He wouldn't run toward a siren, no matter how unpredictable he was. I squeezed back into the seat beside Kay.

"Let's go down this road, Kay."

"Do you think he went that way? That he'll walk clear out of Texas?"

"That's my guess, considering police cars, sirens and other probabilities. Let's go, but take it easy for my headache's sake. Follow Marvin in the car up ahead–but don't get too close."

As we pulled away I caught a glimpse of the girl who tattled on Junior, sobbing away as if all the world's burdens were on her shoulders as she sat hunched forward in Campbell's car. Kay romped on it until we almost caught the police car, then trailed it at about fifty yards.

Marvin and Harry stopped at the first house but they didn't get in to do any looking. The farmer-owner wouldn't let them in because they didn't have a warrant, but they knew him and took his word that Junior wasn't inside. They figured Junior would have needed a warrant himself, or else he'd have had to kill the cantankerous old man who came to the door. The cops got back in their car and started easing down the road again.

We went at a slow crawl. Those cops were being careful. I knew they wanted the credit for trapping Junior but I had a hunch they weren't anxious to tangle with him. They watched the ditches as the Lieutenant had told them, and checked several more houses with no luck, or with good luck—depending upon how they felt about finding Junior.

They came to a house that looked like a natural, to me. Set back from the road with a large lawn to cross before reaching the porch, it had the look of a good place for a man to hide and be able to see all the moves his pursuers made.

"Stop the car here, Kay. Now, back up a bit. Good. We'll watch from here on this one and see how they make out."

It didn't take long to see. Harry was about halfway across the lawn when a shot boomed out from a second-story window. Harry seemed to hesitate a moment, then fell face down in the long grass to lie very, very still. Gravel and sand spewed from under the rear wheels of their car as Marvin left the scene in a hurry and rounded a slight bend to go out of sight.

"Mark one more up for Junior," I said. "Nice to be back here out of range, isn't it?"

I dismounted. Kay stepped down into the road, too.

"What now, Bill? Do we go in after him?"

"Do you think that would be wise? We do not."

"Are you afraid of him?"

"Let's say I'm prudent. We can wait. Marvin'll call for help—and that way the taxpayers' boys can take the chances for us. Besides, we don't have a search-warrant—remember the argument at the first house?"

She snorted. But we waited. And I swore at the pain in my head.

We stood around a few minutes watching and seeing nothing, and I got restless. I walked over to the edge of the ditch and went a few steps in the direction of the house. I wanted to get closer and still stay out of pistol range, and see if I could catch any movement behind the windows to keep our boy located for the hired help I knew would show up any minute. I wasn't close enough yet, so I jumped down in the ditch to crawl nearer.

The jump saved my life.

A shot cracked out just as I jumped, and a slug tugged at my shirt where it billowed out a bit in the back from my sudden movement. I dived face forward in the ditch, chewing the dirt with my teeth. My head was spinning dizzily and I was as scared as an old lady getting a ticket for jay-walking. That shot came from behind me!

I was quiet as the spreading dust while I worked up enough nerve to get my gun out. It took guts to get it and raise my head to the level of the ditch for a look to the rear. Junior had shot at me–though how he got back there I couldn't figure.

I'd hit the ditch so quick and nestled so close into the dirt, he must have thought he'd nailed me good with that one shot.

He was under the steering wheel of the Jaguar now, fumbling with the controls and trying to start the motor. I couldn't see Kay and I hoped Junior had overlooked her in his hurry to get going. Then I saw her come out of the ditch on the other side of the road.

She was holding that little pearl-handled .25-caliber toy in front of her. She walked slowly and deliberately up behind the car and came around to Junior's side. I imagined I could see generations of vengeful, hating Texans living in her set features in that moment. Then she was almost abreast of Junior and he hadn't noticed her. I was too fascinated to move or speak as I watched her personification of the Grim Reaper.

"Junior!" Kay screamed sharply.

Things happened fast.

The midget car's engine roared to life at the same time Junior twisted his head around with a startled look at Kay. He was fascinated, too, but not too much not to go for the gun he'd laid in the seat. He made a quick grab for it as Kay pulled the trigger.

The car jumped forward after the shot, but the engine stalled with no one to feed it fuel. The Jaguar had stopped with one wheel over the edge of the ditch. Junior had stopped with a small hole spreading red dye around itself in the center of his forehead. I came out of my trance and stood up.

Kay walked to the car. She held the gun at four-inch range and carefully spaced four more little holes into Junior's head– working as if by a mental pattern she had prepared long ago, as she pumped the slugs out of her little pistol.

She stood looking down at him. Her face was a hideous mold of stark, fiendish glee as she gazed hungrily at Junior's butchered face, drinking it in with the eyes of a demon gone insanely jubilant.

I shivered, looking at her looking at him. An ice-cold hand was inside my back and around my spine, running up and down giving each separate vertebra a clammy squeeze as it passed. I wished for something to bring that endless minute to an end, and something did.

The siren was coming down the road. Lieutenant Campbell's car with a dustcloud attached behind pulled up to us and stopped. He got out, gun in hand, and took a look at Junior. Seeing his gun, I realized mine had fallen from my hand back in the ditch, but I didn't bother to go after it. I wouldn't need it any more.

"Three down, none to go," the Lieutenant said,

Kay looked at him. That look I never want to see again but will see in my dreams until the day I die was gone. Her face was perfectly composed, with its natural, lovely human look.

"Get that body out of my car, Lieutenant," she said.

Campbell and his driver obliged her. I made no move to help. Kay took off her jacket, wiped the blood from the leather

190

seat of the car, and threw the jacket in the ditch. Then she got into the car.

"Come on, Bill. Let's go back to the house for a drink. It's hot out here in the sun."

"Where'd the girl go, Lieutenant?" I asked.

"I sent her to town for medical care—she went all to pieces listening to the radio calls."

"Well, I guess it's all over. Be seeing you, Lieutenant."

"Sure. By the way, Brown, I hope you can get that Los Angeles harness on again—over your headache, I mean." He laughed at me.

Amazing fellow, that Lieutenant Campbell. I got in the car and Kay backed into the road, turned around and started towards Dallas.

I was set. Here I was, riding with the richest and probably the most beautiful girl in Texas. She was alone in the world and I held the inside track. From the brink of her emotional breakdown I would nurse her back to normalcy, and when things blew over she would be mine. It would be easy to freeze everyone else out. Then—marry the girl. Ranches, with plenty of meat on the hoof. Oil wells, with cash in every barrel. I'd have a house on the Riviera, another in Honolulu, and a beach cottage at Malibu, of course. Once a year I could bring her back to Dallas, and we'd spend a week or so in the bank vault—clipping coupons. I had it all figured out. It was so easy.

Then. The look on her face when she fired the last four shots into Junior's face from close enough to powder-blister him. That stopped me. I shuddered as the memory chased all the pretty visions I'd had right out of my mind.

"Kay," I said. "Would you mind turning back and dropping me at the airport?"

"Why the airport, Bill? Lose something out there?"

"You don't have to. Let me off here—I can hitch a ride."

"No. I don't mind. I'll take you."

The rest of the ride was in silence. She didn't look at me and I didn't look at her. I was afraid to—afraid I'd change my mind. When she pulled up in front of the terminal building I did take a long look at her, and found it was easy.

"Thanks, Kay, for trusting me like you did."

"Where are you going?"

"Away from Dallas, Kay. L. A., maybe. I don't know."

"Would you mind kissing me goodbye, Bill?"

"No. I don't mind."

I did, like I was kissing my mother goodbye on my way to school.

I turned, without looking back, and walked into the terminal building. As I stood in front of the ticket window, I realized something momentous.

My headache was gone! Disappeared. Just like that.

"Los Angeles," I said to the clerk. "One way."

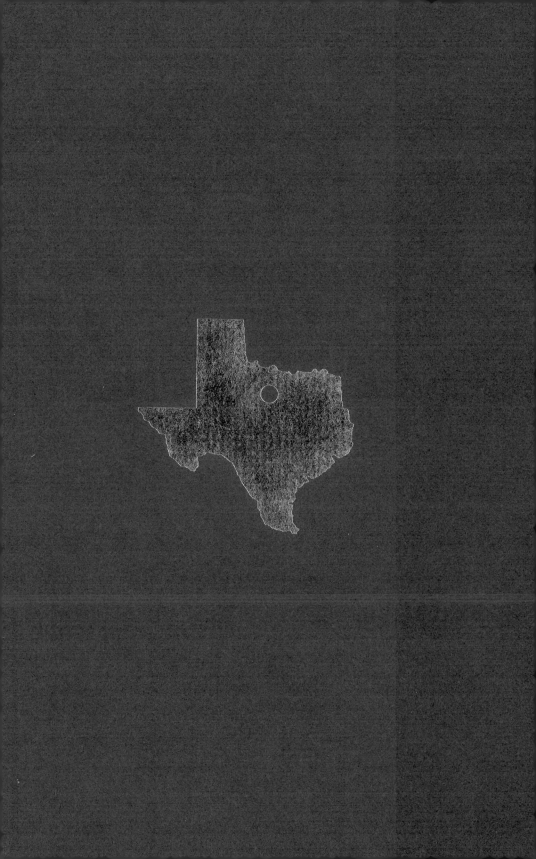